Jewel Whitelaw, one of eight children
adopted by the Whitelaws of Texas,
is a woman now. And she wants to be
introduced to the wonders of passion.
By one man—Mac Macready.

Yes—*the* Mac Macready.

But Mac truly is a living legend in Texas...
for something no one would believe.
Mac Macready is a virgin.
Yes—*that* kind of virgin.
And it's going to be one long,
hot summer....

JOAN JOHNSTON

The Virgin Groom

HAWK'S WAY

Silhouette Books

Published by Silhouette Books

America's Publisher of Contemporary Romance

SILHOUETTE BOOKS

HAWK'S WAY
THE VIRGIN GROOM

Copyright © 1997 by Joan Johnston

ISBN 0-373-48351-1

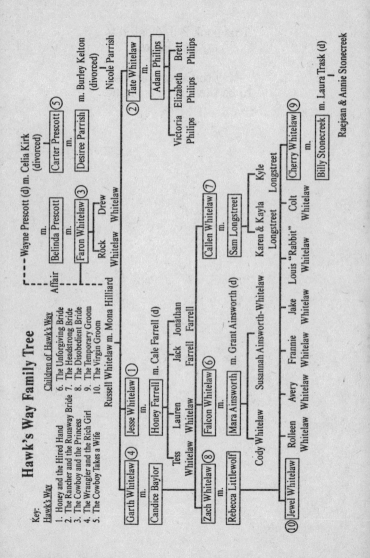

Hawk's Way Family Tree

This book is dedicated to
my son, Blake.

May you always strive
to be the best you can be.

Chapter 1

Sweat streaming from his temples, strong hands clenched tight on the parallel bars that supported him, Mac Macready put his full weight on his left leg. He felt a sharp pain, but the leg held. He gritted his teeth to keep from groaning. So far, so good.

Mac kept his eyes focused on the area between the bars in front of him, willing his leg to work. He took an easy step with his right leg, then called on the left again. The pain was less sharp the second time he put his weight on the restructured limb. He could handle the pain.

More important, the leg had stayed under him. He glanced across the room at his friend and agent, Andy Dennison, and grinned.

Mac Macready could walk again.

"You did it, Mac," Andy said, crossing the room to slap him on the back. "It's great to see you back on your feet."

"About time," Mac said. "I've spent the better part of two years trying to get this damned leg of mine back into shape." A sharp pain seared up his leg, but he refused to sit down, not now, when he had just made it back onto his feet. He took more of his weight on his arms and kept walking. A bead of sweat trickled between his shoulder blades before it caught on his sleeveless T-shirt. He summoned another smile. "Give me a couple of months, and I'll be ready to start catching passes again for the Tornadoes."

Mac caught the skeptical look on Andy's face before his agent said, "Sure, Mac. Whatever you say."

He understood Andy's skepticism. Mac had said the same thing after every operation. Who would have suspected a broken leg—all right, so maybe it had been shattered—would be so difficult to mend? But his body had rejected the pins they had used to put things back together again at ankle and hip. They had finally had to invent something especially for him.

Then the long bones in his leg hadn't grown straight and had needed to be broken and set again. He had fought complications caused by infection. Finally, when he had pushed too hard to get well, he had ended up back in a cast.

The football injury had been devastating, coming as it had at the end of Mac's first phenomenal season with the Texas Tornadoes. His future couldn't have been brighter. He was a star receiver, with more touchdown catches than any other rookie in the league. His team was headed for the Super Bowl. With one crushing tackle, everything had fallen apart. The sportscasters had called it a career-ending injury. Mac wasn't willing to concede the issue.

"Good work, Mac," the physical therapist said, reaching out to help him into the wheelchair waiting for him at the end of the parallel bars. "Put your arm around me."

He flashed the young woman a killer grin, inwardly cursing the fact that after six measly steps he was on the verge of collapse. "Better watch out, Hartwell. Now that I'm back on my feet, I'm going to give your fiancé some serious competition.''

Diane Hartwell blushed. Most women did when Mac turned on the charm. He had the kind of blond-haired, blue-eyed good looks that made female heads swivel to take a second look. Mac wondered what she would think if she knew the truth about him.

Diane answered wryly, ''I'm sure George would gladly trade me to you for an autographed football.''

''Done,'' Mac said brightly, biting back a grimace as Diane bent his injured leg and placed his foot on the wheelchair footrest.

''I was only kidding,'' Diane said.

''I wasn't,'' Mac said, smiling up at her. ''Tell your fiancé I'll be glad to autograph that football for him anytime.''

''Thanks, Mac,'' Diane said. ''I appreciate it.''

''Think nothing of it, Hartwell. And tell George to hang on to that ball. Someday it'll be worth something.''

Once Mac resumed his career, he would break every record in the book. He had that kind of determination. And he had been that good. Of course, that was before the accident. Everybody—except himself—questioned whether he would ever be that good again.

It had been touch and go for a while whether he would even walk. But Mac had known he would walk again, and without the aid of a brace. He had done it today. It seemed he was the only one who wasn't surprised.

He had known he would succeed, because he had beaten the odds before. When he was eight, he had suffered from acute myelocytic leukemia. It should have killed him. He had recovered from the childhood disease and gone on to win the Heisman Trophy and be drafted in the first round by the Texas Tornadoes. Mac had no intention of giving up his dreams of a future in football.

Andy wheeled him down the hospital corridor to his room. "When do you get out of here?" his agent asked.

"The doctor said once I could stand on my leg, he would release me. I guess that means I can get out of here anytime now."

"The press will want a statement," Andy said as he stopped the wheelchair beside Mac's hospital bed. "Do you want to talk to them? Or do you want me to do it?"

Mac thought of facing a dozen TV cameras from a wheelchair. Or standing with crutches. Or wavering on his own two feet. "Tell them I'll be back next season."

"Maybe that's not such a good—"

"Tell them I'll be back," Mac said, staring Andy in the eye.

Andy had once been a defensive lineman and wore a coveted Super Bowl ring on his right hand. He understood what it meant to play football. And what it meant to stop. He straightened the tie at his bull neck, shrugged his broad shoulders and smoothed the tie over his burgeoning belly, before he said, "You got it, Mac."

"Thanks, Andy. I am coming back, you know."

"Sure, Mac," Andy said.

Mac could see his agent didn't believe him any more than the doctors and nurses who had treated him over the past two years. Even Hartwell, though she encouraged him, didn't believe he would achieve the kind of mobility he needed to play in the pros. Mac needed to get away somewhere and heal himself. He knew he could do it. After all, he had done it once before.

"Where can I get in touch with you?" Andy asked.

"I'm headed to a ranch in northwest Texas owned by some friends of mine. I have an open invitation to visit, and I'm going to take them up on it. I'll call you when I get there and give you a number where I can be reached."

"Good enough. Take care, Mac. Don't—"

"Don't finish that sentence, Andy. Not if you're going to warn me not to get my hopes up."

Andy shook his head. "I was going to say don't be a fool and kill yourself trying to get well too fast."

"I'm going to get my job back from the kid who took over for me," Mac said in a steely voice. "And I'm going to do it this year."

Andy didn't argue further, just shook Mac's hand and left him alone in the hospital room.

Mac looked around at the sterile walls, the white sheets, the chrome rails on the bed, listened to the muffled sounds that weren't quite silence and inhaled the overwhelming antiseptic smell that made him want to gag. He had spent too much of his life in hospital beds—more than any human being ought to have to. He wanted out of here, the sooner the better.

He could hardly wait to get to the wide open spaces of Zach and Rebecca Whitelaw's ranch, Hawk's Pride. More than Zach or Rebecca or the land, he had a yearning to see their daughter Jewel again. Jewel was the first of eight kids who had been adopted by the Whitelaws, and she had returned to Hawk's Pride after college to manage Camp LittleHawk, the camp for kids with cancer that Rebecca had started years ago.

Mac remembered his first impressions of Jewel—huge Mississippi-mud-brown eyes, shoulder-length dirt-brown hair and an even dirt-ier looking white T-shirt and jeans. She had been five years old to his eight, and she had been leaning against the corral at Camp LittleHawk watching him venture onto horseback for the first time.

"Don't be scared," Jewel had said.

"I'm not," he'd retorted, glancing around at the other five kids in the corral with him. The horses were stopped in a circle, and the wrangler was working with a little boy who was even more scared than he was.

"Buttercup wouldn't hurt a fly," Jewel reassured him.

He remembered feeling mortified at the thought of riding a horse named Buttercup. And terrified that Buttercup would throw him off her broad back and trample him underfoot. Even though he'd been dying of cancer, he'd been afraid of getting killed. Life, he had learned, was precious.

"I'm not scared," he lied. He wished he could reach up and tug his baseball cap down tighter over his bald head, but he was afraid to let go of his two-handed grip on the saddle horn.

Jewel scooted under the bottom rail of the corral on her hands and knees, which explained how she had gotten so dirty, and walked right up to the horse—all right, it was only a pony, but it was still big—without fear. He sat frozen as she patted Buttercup's graying jaw and crooned to her.

"What are you saying?" he demanded.

"I'm telling Buttercup to be good. I'm telling her you're sick and—"

"I'm dying," he blurted out. "I'll be dead by

Christmas." It was June. He was currently in remission, but the last time he'd been sick, he'd heard the doctors figuring he had about six months to live. He knew it was only a matter of time before the disease came back. It always did.

"My momma died and my daddy and my brother," Jewel said. "I thought I was gonna die, too, but I didn't." She reached up and touched the crisscrossing pink scars on her face. "I had to stay in the hospital till I got well."

"Then you know it's a rotten place to be," he said.

She nodded. "Zach and 'Becca came and took me away. I never want to go back."

"Yeah, well I don't have much choice."

"Why not?" she asked.

"Because that's where you go when you're sick."

"But you're well now," she said, looking up at him with serious brown eyes. "Except you don't have any hair yet. But don't worry. 'Becca says it'll grow back."

He flushed and risked letting go of the horn to tug the cap down. It was one of the many humiliations he had endured—losing his hair...along with his privacy...and his childhood. He had always wanted to go to camp like his sister, Sadie, but he had been too sick. Then some lady had opened this place. He had jumped at the chance to get away from home. Away from the hospital.

"Your hair doesn't grow back till you stop getting sick," he pointed out to the fearless kid standing with her cheek next to the pony's.

"So, don't get sick again," she said.

He snickered. "Yeah. Right. It doesn't work like that."

"Just believe you can stay well, and you will," she said.

The circle of horses began to move again, and she headed back toward the fence. It was then he noticed her limp. "Hey!" he shouted after her. "What happened to your leg?"

"It got broken," she said matter-of-factly.

Mac hadn't thought much about it then, but now he knew the pain she must have endured to walk again. Jewel would know what he was feeling as he got out of the hospital for what he hoped would be the last time. Jewel would understand.

After that first meeting, he and Jewel had encountered each other often over the next several years. He had beaten the leukemia and returned as a teenager to become a counselor at Camp LittleHawk. That was when Jewel had become his best friend. Not his *girlfriend*. His *best friend*.

He already had a girlfriend back home in Dallas. Her name was Louise and he called her Lou and was violently in love with her. He had met Lou when she came to the junior-senior prom with another guy. She had only been in the eighth grade. By the time he was a senior and Lou was a freshman, they were going steady.

He told Jewel all about the agonies of being in love, and though she hadn't yet taken the plunge, she was all sympathetic ears. Jewel was the best buddy a guy could have, a confidante, a pal. A soul mate. He could tell her anything and, in fact, had told her some amazingly private things.

Like how he had cried the first time he had endured a procedure called a back-stick, where they stuck a needle in your back to figure out your blood count. How he had wet the bed once in the hospital rather than ask for a bedpan. And how humiliating it had been when the nurse treated him like a baby and put the thermometer into an orifice other than his mouth.

It was astonishing to think he could have been so frank with Jewel. But Jewel didn't only listen to his woes, she shared her own. So he knew how jealous and angry she had been when Zach and Rebecca adopted another little girl two years older than her named Rolleen. And how she had learned to accept each new child a little more willingly, until the youngest, Colt, had come along, and he had felt like her own flesh-and-blood baby brother.

Mac had also been there at the worst moment of her life. He had lost a good friend that fateful Fourth of July. And Jewel... Jewel had lost much more. After that hot, horrible summer day, she had refused to see him again. So far, he had respected her wish to be left alone. But there was an empty place inside him she had once helped to fill.

He had received an invitation to her wedding the previous spring. It was hard to say what his feelings had been. Joy for her, because he knew how hard it must have been for her to move past what had happened to her. And sadness, too, because he knew the closeness they had enjoyed in the past would be transferred to her husband.

Then had come the announcement, a few weeks before the wedding, that it had been canceled. He had wondered what had gone wrong, wondered which of them had called it off and worried about what she must be feeling. He would never pry, but he was curious. After all, he and Jewel had once known everything there was to know about each other. He had picked up the phone to call her, but put it down. Too many years had passed.

Mac had never had another woman friend like Jewel. Sex always got in the way. Or rather, the woman's expectations. And his inability to fulfill them.

What kind of man is still a virgin at twenty-five? Mac mused.

An angry man. A onetime romantic fool who waited through college for his high school sweetheart to grow up, only to be left for another guy.

It hadn't seemed like such a terrible sacrifice remaining faithful to Louise all those years, turning down girls who showed up at his dorm room in T-shirts and not much else, girls who wanted to make it with a college football hero, girls who were attracted by his calendar-stud good looks. He had loved Lou and had his whole life with her ahead of him.

Until she had jilted him her senior year for Harry Warnecke, who had a bright future running his father's bowling alley.

Lou had been gentle but firm in her rejection of him. "I don't love you anymore, Mac. I love Harry. I'm pregnant, and we're going to be married."

Mac had been livid with fury. He had never touched her, had respected her wish to remain a virgin until she graduated from high school and they could marry, and she was pregnant with some guy named Harry's kid and wanted to marry him.

It had taken every ounce of self-control he had not to reach out and throttle her. "Have a nice life," he had managed to say.

His anger had prodded him to hunt up the first available woman and get laid. But his pain had sent him back to his dorm room to nurse his broken heart. How could he make love to another woman when he still loved Lou? If all he had wanted was to get screwed, he could have been doing that all along. His dad had always told him that sex felt good, but making love felt better. He had wanted it to be making love the first time.

His final year of college, after he broke up with Lou, he went through a lot of women. Dating them, that is. Kissing them and touching them and learning what made them respond to a man. But he never put himself inside one of them. He was looking for something more than sex in the relationship. What he found were women who admired his body, or his talent with a football, or his financial prospects. Not one of them wanted him.

It wasn't until he had been drafted by the pros and began traveling with the Tornadoes that he met Elizabeth Kale. She was a female TV sports commentator, a woman who felt comfortable with jocks and could banter with the best of them. She had taken his breath away. She had shiny brown hair and warm brown eyes and a smile that wouldn't quit. He had fallen faster than a wrestled steer in a rodeo.

She hadn't been impressed by his statistics— personal or football or financial. It had not been easy to get her to go out with him. She didn't want to get involved. She had her career, and marriage wasn't in the picture.

Mac didn't give up when he wanted something—and he'd wanted to marry Elizabeth. As the season progressed, they began to see each other when they were both in town. Elizabeth was a city girl, so they did city things—when they could both fit it into their busy schedules. Mac wooed her with every romantic gesture he could think of, and she responded. And when he proposed marriage, she accepted. Elizabeth made what time she could for him, and they exchanged a lot of passionate kisses at airports where their paths crossed.

He had carefully planned her seduction. He knew when and where it was going to happen. He was nervous and eager and restless. By a certain age—and Mac had already reached it— a woman expected a man to know all the right moves. Mac had been to the goal line plenty of times, but he had never scored a touchdown. He was ready and willing to take the plunge—figuratively speaking—but now that he had waited so long, the idea of making it with a woman for the first time was a little unnerving. Especially with Elizabeth, who meant so much to him.

What if he did it wrong? What if he couldn't please her? What if he left her unsatisfied? He read books. And planned. And postponed the moment.

Then he broke his leg. *Shattered his leg.*

Mac tasted bile in his throat, remembering what had happened next. Elizabeth had come to the hospital to see him, flashbulbs popping around her, as much in the news as his girlfriend as she was as a famous newscaster. She listened at his bedside to the prognosis.

His football career was over. He would be lucky if he ever walked again. He would always need a brace on his leg. Maybe he could manage with a cane.

He had seen it in her eyes before she spoke a word. The fear. And the determination. She said nothing until the doctors had left them alone.

"I can't—I won't—I can't do it, Mac."

"Do what, Elizabeth?" he asked in a bitter voice that revealed he knew exactly what she meant, though he pretended ignorance.

"I won't marry a man who can't walk." She slipped her widespread fingers slowly through the hair that fell forward on her face, carefully settling it back in place. He had always thought it a charming gesture, but now it only made her seem vain.

"I can't go through this with you," she said. "I mean, I...I hate hospitals and sick people and I can't...I can't be there for you, Mac."

He had known it was coming, but it hurt just the same. "Get out, Elizabeth."

She stood there waiting for...what?...for him to tell her it was all right? It wasn't, by God, all right! It was a hell of a thing to tell a man you couldn't stand by him in times of trouble. *For better or for worse.* It told him plenty about just how deep her feelings for him ran. Thin as sheet ice on a Texas pond.

"I said get out!" He was shouting by then, and she flinched and backed away. "Get out!"

She turned and ran.

His throat hurt from shouting and his leg throbbed and his eyes and nose burned with un-shed tears. He shouted at the nurse when she tried to come in, but he couldn't even turn over and bury his head in a pillow because they had his leg so strapped up.

Mac forced his mind away from the painful memories. There had been no seductions during the past two years, though he had spent a great deal of time in bed. He had been too busy trying to get well. Now he was well. And he was going to have to face that zero on the scoreboard and do something about it.

He could find a woman who knew the ropes—there were certainly enough volunteers even now—and get it over with. But he found that a little cold and calculating. The first time ought to be with a special woman. Not that he would ever be stupid enough to fall in love again. After all, twice burned, thrice chary. But he wanted to like and respect and admire the woman he chose as his first sexual partner.

Lately his dreams had been unbelievably erotic. *Hot, sweat-slick bodies entwined in twisted sheets. Long female legs wrapped around his waist. A woman's hair draped across his chest. His mouth on her—* He shook off the vision. Now that he was finally healthy—meaning he could get out of bed as easily as he could fall into it—it was time he took care of unfinished business.

Jewel's face appeared in his mind's eye. He saw the faint, crisscrossing scars from the car accident that had left her an orphan which had never quite faded away. Her smile, winsome and mischievous. Heard the distressed sound of her voice when she admitted her breasts kept growing and growing like two balloons. And her laughter when he had offered to pop them for her.

With Jewel he wouldn't have to be afraid of making a fool of himself in bed. Jewel would understand his predicament. But she was the last person he could ever have sex with. Not after what had happened to her.

He was sure she would see the humor in the current situation. Jewel had a great sense of humor. At least, once upon a time she had. He could hardly believe six years had passed since they had last seen each other. They had both been through a great deal since then.

Mac hoped Jewel wouldn't mind him intruding on her this way. But he was coming, like it or not.

Chapter 2

Peter "Mac" Macready was the last person
Jewel Whitelaw wanted to see back at Hawk's
Pride, because he was the one person besides her
counselor who knew her deepest, darkest secret.
She should have told someone else long ago—
her parents, one of her three sisters or four brothers, her fiancé—but she had never been able to
admit the truth to anyone. Only Mac knew. And
now he was coming back.

If she could have left home while he was visiting, she would have done so. But Camp Little-
Hawk was scheduled to open in two weeks, and

she had too much to do to get ready for the summer season to be able to pick up and leave. All she could do was avoid Mac as much as possible.

As she emerged from a steamy shower, draped herself in a floor-length white terry cloth robe and wrapped her long brown hair in a towel, she learned just how impossible that was going to be.

"Hi."

He was standing at the open bathroom door dressed in worn Levi's, a Tornadoes T-shirt and Nikes, leaning on a cane. He didn't even have the grace to look embarrassed. A grin split his face from ear to ear, creating two masculine dimples in his cheeks, while his vivid blue eyes gazed at her with the warmth of an August day in Texas.

"Hi," she said back. In spite of not wanting him here, she felt her lips curve in an answering smile. Her gaze skipped to the knotty-looking hickory cane he leaned on and back to his face. "I see you're standing on your own."

"Almost," he said. "Sorry about intruding. Your mom said to make myself comfortable." He gestured to the bedroom behind him, on the other side of the bathroom, where his suitcase sat on the double bed. "Looks like we'll be sharing a bath."

Jewel groaned inwardly. The new camp counselors' cottages had been built to match the single-story Spanish style of the main ranch house, with whitewashed adobe walls and a red barrel-tile roof. Each had two bedrooms, but shared a bath, living room and kitchen. As the camp manager, she should have had this cottage all to herself. "I thought you'd be staying at the house," she said.

"Your mom gave me a choice." He shrugged. "This seemed more private."

"I see." Her mother had asked her if she minded, since Jewel and Mac were such old friends, if she gave Mac a choice of staying at the cottage or in the house. Jewel hadn't objected, because she hadn't been able to think up a good reason to say no that wouldn't sound suspicious. As far as her parents knew, she and Mac still were good friends. And they were.

Only, Jewel had expected Mac to keep his distance, as he had for the past six years. And he had not.

Mac's brow furrowed in a way that was achingly familiar. "I can tell Rebecca I've changed my mind, if you don't want me here."

Jewel struggled between the desire to escape Mac's scrutiny and the yearning to have back the camaraderie they had once enjoyed. Maybe it would be all right. Maybe the subject wouldn't come up. *Yeah, and maybe horses come in green and pink.* "I..."

He started to turn away. "I'll get my bag."

"Wait."

He turned back. "I don't want to make you uncomfortable, Jewel. I won't talk about it. I won't even bring up the subject." His lips curled wryly. "Of course, I just brought up the subject to say I won't bring it up, but I promise it'll be off-limits. I need a place to rest and get better, and I thought you might not mind if I stayed here."

His eyes looked wounded, and her heart went out to him. She crossed to him, because that seemed easier than making him walk to her with the cane. His arms opened to her and she walked right into them and they hugged tightly.

"God, I've missed you," he said, his deep voice rumbling in her ear.

"This feels good," she admitted. "It's been too long, Mac."

There was nothing sexual in the embrace, just two old friends, two very good friends, reconnecting after a long separation. Except Jewel was aware of the strength in his arms, the way her breasts felt crushed against his muscular chest and the feel of his thighs pressed against her own. She stiffened, then forced herself to relax.

"You're taller than I remember," he said, tucking her towel-covered head under his chin.

"I've grown three inches since... I've grown," she said, realizing how difficult it was going to be avoiding the subject she wanted to avoid. "It's a good thing, or I'd get a crick in my neck looking up at you."

He had to be four inches over six feet. She remembered him being tall at nineteen, but he must have grown an inch or two since then, and of course his shoulders were broader, his angular features more mature. He was a man now, not a boy.

He was big. He was strong. He could physically overwhelm her. But she had known Mac forever. He would never hurt her. She reminded herself to relax.

The towel slipped off, and her hair cascaded to her waist.

"Good Lord," Mac said, his fingers tangling in the length of it. "Your hair was never this long, either."

"I like it long." She could drape it forward over her shoulders to help cover her Enormous Endowments.

"I think I'm going to like it, too," he said, smiling down at her with a teasing glint in his eyes.

She gave him an arch look. "Are you flirting with me, Mr. Macready?"

"Who, me? Naw. Wouldn't think of it, Ruby."

Jewel grinned. In the old days, he had often called her by the names of different precious gems—"Because you're a Jewel, get it?"—and the return to such familiarity made her feel even more comfortable with him. "Get out of here so I can get dressed," she said, stepping back from his embrace.

The robe gaped momentarily, and his glance slipped downward appreciatively. She self-consciously pulled the cloth over her breasts to cover them completely.

"Looks like they've grown, too," he quipped, leering at her comically.

She should have laughed. It was what she would have done six years ago, before disaster had struck. But she couldn't joke with him anymore about her overgenerous breasts. She blamed the size of them for what had happened to her. "Don't, Mac," she said quietly.

He sobered instantly. "I'm sorry, Jewel."

She managed a smile. "It's no big deal. Just get out of here and let me get dressed."

He backed up, and for the first time she saw how much he needed the cane. His face turned white around the mouth with pain, and he swore under his breath.

"Are you all right?" she asked.

"No problem," he said. "Leg's almost as good as new. Figure I'll start jogging tomorrow."

"Jogging?"

He gave her a sheepish look. "So maybe I'll start out walking. Want to go with me?"

She daintily pointed the toe of her once-injured leg in his direction. "Walking isn't my forte. How about a horseback ride?"

He shook his head. "Gotta walk. Need the exercise to get back into shape. Come with me. My limp is worse than yours, so you won't have any trouble keeping up. Besides, it would give us a chance to catch up on what we've both been doing the past six years. Please come."

She wrinkled her nose.

"Pretty please with sugar on it?"

It was something she had taught him to say if he really wanted a woman to do something. She gave in to the smile and let her lips curve with the delight she felt. "All right, you hopeless romantic. I'll walk with you, but it'll have to be early because I've got a lot of work to do tomorrow."

"Figured I'd go early to beat the heat," he said. "Six-thirty?"

"Make it six, and you've got a deal." She reached out a hand, and Mac shook it.

The electric shock that raced up her arm was disturbing. It took an effort to keep the frown from her face. This wasn't supposed to happen. She wasn't supposed to be physically attracted to Mac Macready. They were just good friends. *Yeah, and horses come in purple and orange.*

She closed the bathroom door and sank onto the edge of the tub. She had always thought Mac was cute, but he had matured into a genuine hunk. No problem. She would handle the attraction the way she had from the beginning, by thinking of him as a brother.

But he wasn't her brother. He was a very attractive, very available man. Who once had been—still was?—her best friend.

She clung to that thought, which made it easier to keep their relationship in perspective. It was much more important to have a friend like Mac than a boyfriend.

Jewel repeated that sentence like a litany the next morning at 5:55 when Mac showed up in the kitchen dressed in Nikes and black running shorts and nothing else. The kitchen door was open and through the screen she was aware of flies buzzing and the lowing of cattle. A steady, squeaking sound meant that her youngest brother, Colt, hadn't gotten around to oiling the windmill beside the stock pond. But those distractions weren't enough to keep her from ogling Mac's body.

A wedge of golden hair on his chest became a line of soft down as it reached his navel and disappeared beneath his shorts. She consciously forced her gaze upward.

Mac's tousled, collar-length hair was a sun-kissed blond, and his eyes were as bright as the morning sky. He hadn't shaved, and the overnight beard made him look both dangerous and sexy.

Without the concealing T-shirt and jeans, she could see the sinewy muscles in his shoulders and arms, the washboard belly and the horrible mishmash of scars on his left leg. He leaned heavily on the cane.

She poured him a bowl of cornflakes and doused them with milk. "Eat. You're running late."

"Oh, that I were running," he said. "I'm afraid walking is the best I can do." He hobbled across the redbrick tile floor to the small wooden table, settled himself in the ladderback chair opposite her and began consuming cereal at an alarming rate.

"What's that you're wearing?" he asked.

She tugged at her bulky, short-sleeved sweatshirt, dusted off her cutoff jeans and readjusted her hair over her shoulders. "Some old things."

"Gonna be hot in that," he said between bites.

But the sweatshirt disguised her Bountiful Bosom, which was more important than comfort. "Hungry?" she inquired, her chin resting on her hand as she watched him eat ravenously.

"I missed supper last night."

She had checked his bedroom and found him asleep at suppertime and hadn't disturbed him. He had slept all through the afternoon and evening. "You must have been tired."

"I was. Completely exhausted. Not that I'd admit that to anyone but you." He poured himself another bowl of cereal, doused it with the milk she had left on the table and began eating again.

"Nothing wrong with your appetite," she observed.

He made a sound, but his mouth was too full to answer.

She watched him eat four bowls of cereal. That was about right—two for dinner and two for breakfast. "Ready to go walking now?" she asked.

"Sure." He took his dish to the sink and reached back for hers, which she handed to him.

Seeing the difficulty he was having trying to do everything one-handed, so he could hang on to his cane, she said, "I can do that for you."

"I'm not a cripple!" When he turned to snap at her, he lost his one-handed grip on the dishes. His cane fell as he lurched to catch the bowls with both hands. Without the cane, his left leg crumpled under him.

"Look out!" Jewel cried.

The dishes crashed into the sink as Mac grabbed hold of the counter to keep from falling backward.

"Damn it all to hell!" he raged.

Jewel reached out to comfort him, but he snarled, "Don't touch me. Leave me alone."

Jewel had whirled to leave, when he bit out, "Don't go."

She stopped where she was, but she wanted to run. She didn't want to see his pain. It reminded her too much of her own.

He stared out the window over the sink at the endless reaches of Hawk's Pride, with its vast, grassy plains and the jagged outcroppings of rock that marked the entrance to the canyons in the distance.

"It must be awful," she whispered, "to lose so much."

His eyes slid closed, and she watched his Adam's apple bob as he swallowed hard. He slowly opened his eyes and turned to look at her over his shoulder. "This...the way I am... It's just temporary. I'll be back as good as new next season."

"Will you?"

He met her gaze steadily. "Bet on it."

She knew him too well. Well enough to hear the sheer bravado in his answer and to see the unspoken fear in his eyes that his football career was over. They had always been deeply attuned to one another. He was vulnerable again, in a way he once had been as a youth—this time not to death itself, but to the death of his dreams.

"What can I do, Mac?"

He managed a smile. "Hand me my cane, will you?"

It was easier to do as he asked than to probe the painful issues that he was refusing to address. She crossed to pick up his cane and watched as he eased his weight off his hands and onto his leg with the cane's support.

"Are you sure it isn't too soon to be doing so much?" she asked as he hissed in a breath.

He headed determinedly for the screen door. "The only way my leg can get stronger is if I walk on it."

She followed after him, as she had for nearly a dozen years in their youth. "All right, cowboy. Head 'em up, and move 'em out."

He flashed her his killer grin, and she smiled back, letting the screen door slam behind her.

It was easier to pretend nothing was wrong. But she could already see that things were different between them. They had both been through a great deal in the years since they had last seen each other. She knew as well as he did what it felt like to live with fear, and with disappointment.

She had worked hard to put behind her what had happened the summer she was sixteen and Harvey Barnes had attacked her at the Fourth of July picnic. But even now the memory of that day haunted her.

She had been excited when Harvey, a senior who ran with the in crowd, asked her to the annual county-wide Fourth of July celebration. She'd had a crush on him for a long time, but he hadn't given her a second glance. During the previous year, her breasts had blossomed and given her a figure most movie stars would have paid good dollars to have. A lot of boys stared, including Harvey.

She had suspected why Harvey had asked her out, but she hadn't cared. She had just been so glad to be asked, she had accepted his invitation on the spot.

"Why would you want to go out with a guy who's so full of himself?" Mac asked after she introduced him to Harvey. "I'd be glad to take you." As he had previously, every year he'd been at Hawk's Pride.

"I might as well go with one of my brothers as go with you," she replied. "Harvey's cool. He's a hunk. He's—"

"Yeah, yeah, yeah. I get the message," he said, then teased in a singsong voice, "Pearl's got a boyfriend, Pearl's got a boyfriend."

She aimed a playful fist at his stomach to shut him up, but the truth was, she was hoping the picnic date with Harvey, their first, would lead to a steady relationship.

Mac caught her wrist to protect his belly and said, "All right, go with Harvey Barnes and have a good time. Forget all about me—"

Jewel laughed and said, "That mournful face isn't going to make any difference. I'm still going with Harvey. I'll see you at the picnic. We just won't spend as much time together."

Mac looked down at her, his brow furrowed. He opened his mouth to say something and shut it again.

"What is it?" she asked, seeing how troubled he looked.

"Just don't let him... If he does anything... If you think he's going to..."

"What?" she asked in exasperation.

He let go of her hands to shove both of his through his hair. "If you need help, just yell, and I'll be there."

He had already turned to walk away when she grabbed his arm and turned him back around. "What is it you think Harvey's going to do to me that's so terrible?"

"He's going to want to kiss you," Mac said.

"I want to kiss him back. So what's the problem?"

"Kissing's not the problem," Mac pointed

out. "It's what comes after that. The touching and…and the rest. Sometimes it's not easy for a guy to stop. Not that I'm saying he'd try anything on a first date, but some guys… And with a body like yours…"

Her face felt heated from all the blood rushing to it. Over the years they had managed not to talk seriously about such intimate subjects. Mac never brought them up except in fun, and until recently she hadn't been that interested in boys. She searched his face and found he looked as confused and awkward discussing the subject as she felt.

"How would you know?" she asked. "I mean, about it being hard to stop. Have you done it with Lou?"

His flush deepened. "You know I wouldn't tell you that, even if I had."

"Have you?" she persisted.

He tousled her hair like a brother and said, "Wouldn't you like to know!"

In the days before the picnic, Mac teased her mercilessly about her plan to wear a dress, since she only wore jeans and a T-shirt around the ranch.

Her eldest sister, Rolleen, had agreed to make

a pink gingham dress for her, copying a spaghetti-strapped dress pattern that Jewel loved, but which she couldn't wear because her large breasts needed the support of a heavy-duty bra. Rolleen created essentially the same fitted-bodice, bare-shouldered, full-skirted dress, but made the shoulder straps an inch wide so they would hide her bra straps.

On the day of the picnic, Jewel donned the dress and tied up her shoulder-length hair in a ponytail with a pink gingham bow. Her newest Whitelaw sibling, fifteen-year-old Cherry, insisted that she needed pink lipstick on her lips, which Cherry applied for her with the expertise of one who had been wearing lipstick since she was twelve.

Then Jewel headed out the kitchen door to find Mac, who was driving her to the picnic grounds to meet Harvey.

"Wow!" Mac said when he saw her. "Wow!"

Jewel found it hard to believe the admiration she saw in Mac's eyes. She had long ago accepted the fact she wasn't pretty. She had sun-streaked brown hair and plain brown eyes and extraordinarily ordinary features. Her body was fit and healthy, but faint, crisscrossing scars laced her face, and she had a distinctive permanent limp.

The look in Mac's eyes made her feel radiantly beautiful.

She held out the gingham dress and twirled around for him. "Do you think Harvey will like it?"

"Harvey's gonna love it!" he assured her. "You look good enough to eat. I hope this Harvey character knows how lucky he is." The furrow reappeared on his brow. "He better not—"

She put a finger on the wrinkles in his forehead to smooth them out. "You worry too much, Mac. Nothing bad is going to happen."

Looking back now, Jewel wished she had listened to Mac. She wished she hadn't tried to look so pretty for Harvey Barnes. She wished...

Jewel had gotten counseling in college to help her deal with what had happened that day. The counselor had urged her to tell her parents, and when she had met Jerry Cain and fallen in love with him her junior year at Baylor, the counselor had urged her to tell Jerry, too.

She just couldn't.

Jerry had been a graduate student, years older

than she was, and more mature than the other college boys she had met. He had figured out right away that she was self-conscious about the size of her breasts, and it was his consideration for her feelings that had first attracted her to him. It had been easy to fall in love with him. It had been more difficult—impossible—to trust him with her secret.

Jerry had been more patient with her than she had any right to expect. She had loved kissing him. Been more anxious—but finally accepting—of his caresses. They were engaged before he pressed her to sleep with him. They had already sent out the wedding invitations by the time she did.

It had been a disaster.

They had called off the wedding.

That was a year ago. Jewel had decided that if she couldn't marry and have kids of her own, she could at least work with children who needed her.

So she had come back to Camp LittleHawk.

"Hey. You look like you're a million miles away."

Jewel glanced around and realized she could

hardly see the white adobe ranch buildings, they had walked so far. "Oh. I was thinking."

"To tell you the truth, I enjoyed the quiet company." Sweat beaded Mac's forehead and his upper lip. He winced every time he took a step.

"Haven't we gone far enough?" she asked.

"The doctor said I can do as much as I can stand."

"You look like you're there already," she said.

"Just a little bit farther."

That attitude explained why Mac had become the best at what he did, but Jewel worried about him all the same. "Just don't expect me to carry you back," she joked.

Mac shot her one of his dimpled smiles and said, "Tell me what you've been doing with yourself lately."

"I've been figuring out the daily schedule for Camp LittleHawk."

"Need any help?"

She gave him a surprised look. "I'd love some. Do you have the time?"

He shrugged. "Don't have anything else

planned. What kinds of things are you having the kids do these days?''

She told him, unable to keep the excitement from her voice. ''Horseback riding, picnics and hayrides, of course. And handicrafts, naturally.

''But I've come up with something really exciting this year. We're going to have art sessions at the site of those primitive drawings on the canyon wall here at Hawk's Pride. Once the kids have copied down all the various symbols, we're going to send them off to an archaeologist at the state university for interpretation.

''When her findings are available, I'll forward a copy of them to the kids, wherever they are. It'll remind them what fun they had at camp even after they've gone.''

''And maybe take their minds off their illness, if they're back in the hospital,'' Mac noted quietly.

Jewel sat silently watching Mac stare into the distance and knew he was remembering how it had been in the beginning, how they had provided solace to each other, a needed word of encouragement and a shoulder to lean on. She knew he had come back because she was here, a friend when he needed one.

"I can remember being fascinated by those drawings myself as a kid," Mac mused.

"Didn't you want to be an archaeologist once upon a time?"

"Paleontologist," he corrected.

"What's the difference?"

"An archaeologist studies the past by looking at what people have left behind. A paleontologist studies fossils to recreate a picture of life in the past."

"What happened to those plans?" she asked.

"It got harder and harder to focus on the past when I realized I was going to have a future."

"What college degree did you finally end up getting?"

He laughed self-consciously. "Business. I figured I'd need to know how to handle all the money I'd make playing football."

But his career had been cut short.

He turned abruptly and headed back toward the ranch without another word to her.

Jewel figured the distance they had come at about a mile. She looked at her watch. Six-thirty. Not very far or very fast for a man who depended on his speed for a living.

About a quarter of a mile from the house, Mac

was using his hand to help move his left leg. Jewel stepped to his side and slipped her arm around his waist to help support his weight.

"Don't argue," she said, when he opened his mouth to protest. "If you want my company, you have to take the concern that comes along with it."

"Thanks, Opal," he said.

"Think nothing of it, Pete."

She hadn't called him Pete since he had started high school and acquired the nickname "Mac" from his football teammates. It brought back memories of better times for both of them. They were content to walk in silence the rest of the way back to the house.

Jewel had forgotten how good it felt to have a friend with whom you could communicate without saying a word. She knew what Mac was feeling right now as though he had spoken the words aloud. She understood his frustration. And his fear. She empathized with his drive to succeed, despite the obstacles he had to overcome. She understood his reluctance to accept her help and his willingness to do so.

It was as though the intervening years had never been.

Except, something else had been added to the mix between them. Something unexpected. Something as unwelcome as it was undeniable.

No *friend* should have felt the frisson of excitement Jewel had felt with her body snuggled up next to Mac's. No *friend* should have gotten the chill she got down her spine when Mac's warm breath feathered over her temple. No *friend's* heart would have started beating faster, as hers had, when Mac's arm circled her waist in return, his fingers closing on her flesh beneath the sweatshirt.

She would have to hide what she felt from him. Otherwise it would spoil everything. Friendship had always been enough in the past. Because of what had happened, because she was in no position to ask for—or accept—more, friendship was all they could ever have between them now.

As they reached the kitchen door, she smiled up at Mac, and he smiled back.

"Home again, home again, jiggety jog," she said.

"Same time tomorrow?"

She started to refuse. It would be easier if she kept her distance from him. But it was foolish to deny herself his friendship because she felt more than that for him.

She gave him a cheery smile and said, "Sure. Same time tomorrow." She breathed a sigh of relief that she wouldn't have to face him again for twenty-four hours.

"As soon as I shower, we can go to work planning all those activities for the kids," he said.

Jewel gave him a startled look.

"Changed your mind about wanting my help?"

She had forgotten all about it. "No. I...uh..."

He tousled her hair. "You can make up your mind while I shower. I'll be here if you need me."

A moment later he had disappeared into the house. It was only then she realized he was going to use up all the hot water.

"Hey!" she yelled, yanking the screen door open to follow after him. "I get the shower first!"

He leaned his head out of the bathroom door. She saw a length of naked flank and stopped in her tracks.

"You can have it first tomorrow," he said.

His eyes twinkled as he added, "Unless you'd like to share?"

She put her hand flat on his bare chest, feeling the crisp, sweat-dampened curls under her palm, and shoved him back inside. "Go get cleaned up, stinky," she said, wrinkling her nose. "We've got work to do."

He saluted her and stepped back inside.

It was the right response. Just enough teasing and playful camaraderie to disguise her shiver of delight—and the sudden quiver of fear—at being invited to share Mac's shower.

Chapter 3

"Wow! Mac Macready in the flesh!"

Mac felt embarrassed and humbled at the look of admiration—almost adulation—in Colt Whitelaw's eyes. Mac had just shoved open the kitchen screen door to admire the sunrise on his third day at Hawk's Pride when he encountered Jewel's fourteen-year-old brother on the back steps. He had known the boy since Colt came to the Whitelaw household as an infant, the only one of the eight Whitelaw kids who had known no other parents than Zach and Rebecca. "Hi there, kid."

Colt was wearing a white T-shirt cut off at the waist to expose his concave belly and ribs and with the arms ripped out to reveal sinewy biceps. Levi's covered his long, lanky legs. He was tossing a football from hand to hand as he shifted from foot to booted foot. With the soft black down of adolescence growing on his upper lip, he looked every bit the eager and excited teenager he was.

"Mom said you were coming, but I didn't really believe her. I mean, now that you're famous and all, I didn't think you'd ever come back here. I wanted to come over as soon as you got here, but Mom said you needed time to settle in without all of us bothering you, so I stayed away a whole extra day. I'm not bothering you, am I?"

Mac resisted the urge to ruffle Colt's shaggy, shoulder-length black hair. The kid wouldn't appreciate it. Mac knew from his own experience that a boy of fourteen considered himself pretty much grown up. Colt was six feet tall, but his shoulders were still almost as narrow as his hips. His blue eyes were filled with wonder and hope, without the cynicism and disappointment that appeared as you grew older and learned that life threw a lot of uncatchable balls your way.

"Sit down and tell me what you've been doing with yourself," Mac invited. He eased himself into one of the two slatted white wooden chairs situated on the flagstone patio at the back of the cottage. Colt perched on the wide arm of the other chair.

The patio was arbored, and purple bougainvillea woven within a white lattice framework provided shade to keep the early morning sun off their heads and a pleasant floral fragrance.

Mac was aware of Colt's scrutiny as he gently picked up his wounded leg and set the ankle on the opposite knee. When he was done, he laid his cane down on the flagstone and leaned back comfortably in the chair.

"I was watching the game on TV when your leg got busted," Colt said. "It looked pretty bad."

"It was," Mac agreed.

"I heard them say you'd never walk again," Colt blurted.

Mac managed a smile. "Looks like they were wrong."

"When you didn't come back after a whole year, they said you'd never play football again."

"It's taken me a while to get back on my feet,

but I expect to be back on the football field in the fall as good as new and better than ever."

"Really?" Colt asked.

Mac was fresh out of the shower after his second morning of walking with Jewel, and wished now he had put on jeans and boots instead of shorts and Nikes. The kid was gawking at his scarred leg like he was a mutant from the latest horror movie.

Mac figured it was time to change the subject, or he'd end up crying his woes to the teenager. He gestured to the football in Colt's hands and said, "Are you on the football team at school?"

Colt made a disparaging face and mumbled, "Yeah. I'm the quarterback."

Most boys, especially in Texas, would have been ecstatic at the thought of being quarterback. "It sounds as if you don't care much for football."

"It's all right. It's just..." Colt slid off the arm backward into the slatted wooden chair, with his legs dangling over the arm, the football cradled in the notch of his elbow. "Did you always know what you wanted to do with your life?"

Mac nodded. He had always known he wanted to play football. He just hadn't been sure his body would give him the chance. "How about you?"

"I know exactly what I want to do," Colt said. "I just don't think I'm going to get the chance to do it."

"Why not?"

"Dad expects me to stay here and be a rancher."

"Is that so bad?"

"It is when I'd rather be doing something else."

Mac stared at Colt's troubled face. "Anything you'd like to talk about?"

Colt shrugged. "Naw. I guess not." He settled his feet on the ground and rose with an ease that Mac envied. "Guess I'd better get going. Now that school's out for the summer, I've got a lot of chores to do."

Mac turned his eyes in the direction of the squealing windmill.

Colt laughed. "I'll get to it right away. Hope it hasn't been keeping you awake."

"I've slept fine." Like the dead. He had slept straight through the afternoon and evening of his first day here, and yesterday he had been exhausted after a day spent mostly sitting down, working out a crafts program for the camp with

Jewel. He knew his body needed rest to heal, but he was tired of being tired. He wanted to be well again.

Colt began loping away, then suddenly turned and threw the football in Mac's direction. Instinctively, Mac reached out to catch it. His fingertips settled on the well-thrown ball with remembered ease, and he drew it in.

Colt came loping back, a wide grin splitting his face. "Guess you haven't lost your touch." He held out his hand for the ball.

Mac looked up at the kid, an idea forming in his head. "How would you like to throw a few to me over the next couple of weeks, after I get a little more mobile?"

Colt's eyes went wide with wonder. "You mean it? Really? Hot damn, that would be great! I mean, golly, that would be great!" he quickly corrected himself, looking over his shoulder to see if any of his family had heard him. "Just say when and where."

"Let's say two weeks from today," Mac said. "I'll come and find you."

Colt eyed Mac's injured leg. "Are you sure—"

"Two weeks," Mac said certainly.

Colt grinned. "You got it." He took the ball and sauntered off toward the barn.

Mac let out a deep sigh. He had given himself two weeks to get back enough mobility to be able to run for a pass, when it was taking him thirty minutes to walk a mile.

He turned as he heard the screen door slam and saw Jewel. She was just out of the shower, having been second again this morning, since she had gotten a phone call the instant they came back in the door from their walk. She must have blown her hair dry, because it looked shiny and soft enough for him to want to put his hands in it.

The only time he had ever touched her hair in the past was to tousle it like an older brother or tug on her ponytail. He couldn't help wondering what it would feel like to have all that long, silky hair draped over his body.

Mac turned away. *This is Jewel. Your best friend. You'd better get laid soon, old buddy. You're starting to have really weird fantasies.*

She was wearing jeans and boots and a long-sleeved man's button-down, oxford-cloth shirt turned up at the cuffs with the tails hanging out. He wondered if the shirt had belonged to her fiancé and felt jealous of the man. Which was stupid, because Mac and Jewel had never been lovers.

Would you like to be?

He forced his mind away from that insidious thought. It would mess up everything if he made a move on his best friend. He needed Jewel's friendship too much to spoil things that way.

The shirt was big and blousy on her, and she wore her hair pulled over her shoulders in front to hide whatever there might have been left to see of her figure, which wasn't much.

He started to say "You look great!" and bit his tongue. It sounded too much like something a man might say to a woman he wanted to impress. "Hi," he said instead. "Hope you had enough hot water."

"Barely. I made it a quick shower. I'm definitely first tomorrow." She took the seat next to him, leaned back and inhaled a breath of flower-scented air that made her breasts rise under the shirt. The sight took his breath away.

Whenever he had thought about Jewel in the years they had been apart, it was her laughter he had remembered. The way her eyes crinkled at the corners and her lips curved, revealing even white teeth, and how the sound would kind of bubble up out of her, as effervescent as sparkling water.

He couldn't imagine why he hadn't remembered her breasts. He could see why a man might stare. Had they been that large six years ago? They must have been, or close to it, because he had joked with her about them a lot, he remembered. And she had laughed in response, that effervescent, sparkling laugh.

He realized he hadn't heard her laugh once since he had arrived. She had smiled, but her eyes had never joined her mouth. A sadness lingered, memories of more than uncatchable balls. More like forfeited games.

"Who was that on the phone?" he asked.

"Mrs. Templeton. Her eight-year-old son, Brad, is supposed to be a camper during the first two-week session, but he was having second thoughts about coming."

"Why?"

"She's not really sure. He was excited at first when his parents suggested the camp. She wanted me to talk to him."

"Were you able to change his mind?"

Her lips curved. "Brad's an avid football fan. I mentioned you were here—"

"You shouldn't have done that," Mac said brusquely.

She looked as if he'd kicked her in the stomach. "I'm sorry," she said. "I didn't think you'd mind. You always seemed to like spending time with the kids."

He made a face. "It isn't that I mind spending time with them. It's just—" He didn't want them to see him hobbling around with a cane. He didn't want them feeling sorry for him. He didn't want to be asked a lot of questions for which he had no answers.

He would know in the next few weeks whether his leg was going to stand up to the rigors of running. He wanted time by himself to deal with his disappointment—if that was what it turned out to be. He wanted to be able to rage against fate without worrying about some sick kid's feelings.

"I'm sorry, Mac," Jewel said, reaching out to lay her hand on his forearm.

The hairs on his arms prickled at her touch, and his body responded in a way that both surprised and disturbed him. He resisted the urge to jerk his hand away. That would only hurt her again.

This is Jewel. My friend. There's nothing sexual intended by her touch.

Jewel might be his friend, but his body also recognized her as female. This sort of thing— unwanted arousal—had happened once or twice when they were teenagers, and she had touched him at an odd moment when he wasn't expecting it, but he had always attributed those incidents to randy teenage hormones. That excuse wouldn't work now.

All right, so she was an attractive woman.

That excuse wouldn't work either. Jewel wasn't pretty. Never had been. Her nose was straight and small, her chin was square, her mouth was a bit too big and her eyes were Mississippi-mud brown. Ordinary features all. She did have an extraordinary body. Her long legs, small waist and ample breasts were the stuff of male dreams. But Mac was offended on Jewel's behalf to think that any man could want her because of her body and not because of who she was inside.

So, it's her mind you find attractive?

As a teenager, he had liked her sense of humor, her enthusiasm for life and her willingness to reach out to others. He hadn't seen much of the first two traits this time around, and he wasn't sure whether it was a continued willingness to reach out to others that had made her return to Camp LittleHawk or, as he suspected, a desire to retreat from the world.

Mac had no explanation for his response to Jewel except that he had been celibate for too long. What had happened when Jewel touched him was merely the healthy response of a male animal to a female of the species. The problem would be solved when he found himself a woman and satisfied the simple physiological need that had been too long denied. Which meant he had better make a trip into town sometime soon and find a willing woman.

"Do you want me to call the Templetons back and tell them your plans have changed and you won't be here, after all?" Jewel asked.

He shook his head. "I guess it won't hurt me to be nice to one little boy."

"If you'd rather not—"

"I said I would." He slid his leg off his knee and reached for his cane. "It's not that big a deal, Jewel."

She rose and reached for his arm to help him up.

He jerked away. "I'm not an invalid. I wish you'd stop trying to help me."

He saw the hurt look on her face, but that was better than having her know the sharp sexual response her touch had provoked. That would ruin everything. Better to have her think he was in a lousy mood than find out that he wanted to suck on her breasts or put his hand between her legs and seek the damp heat there.

"I'm going in to town today," he said, realizing he'd better get away for a while and cool down.

"Perfect! I need some things from the hardware store. Could you give me a lift?"

Thank God she wasn't looking at him, or she would have known something was wrong. He opened his mouth to refuse and said, "Sure. Why not? Give me a chance to change into a shirt and jeans and some boots first."

She gave him a blazing smile that made his groin pull up tight. Hell. He'd better find himself a woman. And soon.

No doubt about it, Jewel thought. Mac had been acting strange all day. Every errand he had run had taken him to the opposite end of town from her. Although they had made plans to meet for lunch at the Stanton Hotel Café, he hadn't arrived until she was nearly finished eating. She was sitting on one of the 1950's chrome seats at the lunch counter when he finally showed up, grabbed a cup of coffee, said he wasn't hungry, remembered something else he had to do in town and took off again.

If Jewel hadn't known better, she would have said he didn't want to be anywhere near her. But that was silly. They were best friends.

They had agreed to meet in the parking lot near the bank at four o'clock where Mac had parked his extended cab Chevy pickup and head back to Hawk's Pride. Jewel was sitting on the fender of the truck when Mac finally returned.

"You could have sat inside," he said. "It wasn't locked."

"It was too hot with the windows rolled up, and I needed a key to get them down," she said, lifting the hair at her nape to catch the late afternoon breeze. She heard him suck in a breath and had turned in his direction when a female voice distracted them both.

"Peter? Is that you?"

Jewel rose and turned at the same time as Mac to find a red-headed, green-eyed woman standing beside the bed of the pickup.

"Eve?" Mac replied in tones of astonishment that rivaled the woman's.

She ran toward him, and Jewel watched in awe as Mac dropped his cane to surround the woman with his arms. Jewel hurried to pick it up, certain Mac would lose his balance and need it at any moment.

Only he didn't.

Either he was stronger on his feet than he had been two days ago, or the petite redhead was stronger than she looked.

"Peter. Peter," the woman said, her gaze searching his face.

"Eve. I can't believe it's you!" he replied, his eyes searching her face with equal delight.

He suddenly looked around for Jewel and reached out a hand to draw her closer. "Jewel, this is Evelyn Latham. Eve and I dated for a while in college. She's the only person I ever let get away with calling me Peter."

Eve simpered. "It's because you have such a big—"

"Yeah," Mac cut her off. "Eve, this is my friend, Jewel Whitelaw. I'm spending some time at her parents' ranch."

Jewel saw Eve take one look at her plain face and her unshapely clothes and dismiss her as no competition.

Eve then gave Mac a quick, but thorough, once-over. "You look *purrr*fectly fit to me."

Jewel cringed at the way the woman drew out the word with her Texas accent. Eve obviously appreciated Mac's assets—one of which she had apparently seen up close and personal—and the sexual invitation she extended was clear, at least to Jewel.

Mac must have heard it, too. "What are you doing with yourself these days, Eve? I haven't seen you since…when was it?"

"Graduation day from UT, two years ago."

He looked for a ring on her left hand, but didn't find one. "I thought you were going to marry Joe Bob Struthers."

"I only told you that because I was mad at you for dumping me after only three dates…just when we were getting to know each other so well."

He's probably slept with her, Jewel thought. She couldn't fault Mac's taste. The woman was gorgeous. She wore a clingy green St. John knit dress, with a fashionable gold chain draped across her flat stomach.

Mac gave Eve a look that suggested he would be happy to pick up where they had left off. "So you're not a married woman?"

"I'm free as a bird," Eve confirmed.

"I thought you were a Dallas girl, born and bred. What are you doing out here in the far reaches of northwest Texas?" Mac asked.

"My dad bought the bank here in town. I've been the assistant manager for the past year."

"I never expected any less of you," Mac said, "graduating the way you did at the top of the class."

Pretty *and* smart. That was a lethal combination, Jewel thought. Not that Jewel was competing in any way with Evelyn Latham for Mac's affection. She and Mac were just friends. But she couldn't help thinking that if Mac got involved with Eve, she would see a whole lot less of him, and she did enjoy his company.

"What are you doing here?" Eve asked Mac in return. "Aren't you supposed to be off playing football, or something like that?"

Jewel couldn't believe the woman had dated Mac but had no idea when the football season began and ended.

"It's the off-season," Mac said with an indulgent smile. For the first time it must have occurred to him that he didn't have his cane. He looked around for it, and Jewel handed it to him.

He took it and leaned on it. "I'm here visiting friends and recuperating from a football injury."

"You were hurt?" Eve asked.

Jewel rolled her eyes. Mac gave her a nudge with his hip, and she straightened up.

"You could say that," Mac said. "I guess you didn't hear about it."

Eve turned her mouth down in a delightful moue. "As you very well know I never cared much for football, only for the way you looked in those tight pants."

The sexual innuendo was even more blatant this time, and Jewel felt uncomfortable standing there listening to it. "Sorry we can't stay," she said. "Mac was just giving me ride home."

The pout that appeared on Eve's face would have looked right at home on a three-year-old. "Oh, Mac. I was hoping you'd have dinner with me."

"I still can," Mac said. "I'll take Jewel home and come back. What time and where?"

"How about eight o'clock? My house." She gave Mac an address in the newest condominium complex in town.

Mac grinned. "I'll be there."

"Don't dress up," Eve purred. "I want you to be comfortable."

"You got it," Mac said.

With Jewel standing right there, Eve went up on tiptoe and gave Mac a kiss right on the mouth. Jewel noticed Mac's arm went around her waist quick enough to draw her close, so the kiss wasn't unwelcome. It went on a long time, and from the way their mouths shifted, their tongues were involved.

Jewel stood frozen, unable to move. At last the kiss broke, and Mac shot her a quick, embarrassed look. It was too little, too late. He should have thought of her feelings before he practically made love to another woman right in front of her.

Only it shouldn't have mattered if he kissed somebody else. They were only friends.

"See you at eight," Mac said as he backed away from Eve.

"I'll be waiting," Eve said in a sultry voice.

Mac went around to his side of the truck without stopping to open Jewel's door. Not that she needed her door opened for her. She got in and sat near the edge of the seat, opening the window as soon as Mac started the truck and sticking her elbow out.

"Sorry about that," he said after a few

minutes. "I shouldn't have embarrassed you like that."

"I wasn't embarrassed," Jewel said. "Kiss all the girls you want. It doesn't make any difference to me."

"All right. If that's the way you feel. Just so you don't worry, I may not be back tonight."

"Thanks for telling me," Jewel said. "I won't wait up for you."

She really didn't care. He was just a friend. He'd had another girlfriend most of the time she had known him. This was no different. Except, the whole time she had watched Mac kissing Eve the most stunning thought had been running through her head.

I wish it were me.

Chapter 4

Mac went to Evelyn Latham's house with one purpose in mind: to get laid. Eve opened the door wearing a clingy red velour jumpsuit that sent a wake-up call to his body. He was sure all it would take was one kiss to get the old machinery back into action. So he pulled her into his arms and kissed her and…nothing. Not a damned thing happened.

He worried about the situation all through supper and all through the glass of merlot they enjoyed by the fire he started for her in the stone fireplace. When they ended up entwined on the couch, he willed his body to react to the feel of her lips against his, to the feel of her body beneath his hands. He felt the sweat pop out on his forehead. But...nothing.

This wasn't supposed to happen. Just because he hadn't made love with a woman didn't mean that he didn't want to. He wanted to, all right. His damned body just wasn't cooperating! He made up some excuse for why he couldn't stay—his aching leg had come in handy for once—and bolted.

He drove around for two hours wondering if he was going to spend the rest of his life a virgin. What the hell had gone wrong? He hadn't been able to figure it out but had finally conceded that driving around all night wasn't going to give him any answers.

Then he remembered he had told Jewel he would probably be out all night. What was she going to think if he came back early?

That you don't take your time.

Yeah. Probably she'd just think he'd gotten his fill of Eve already. He couldn't imagine getting his fill of Jewel in bed. The thought of touching her skin, the feel of her hair against his body, the smell of her.

His body stirred in response.

It's too late, buddy. You already missed the party. You have to do that when there's a flesh-and-blood woman around.

And when it was some other woman besides Jewel. It wasn't going to do him any good getting aroused by thoughts of her, because she was the last person he could have sex with.

Hell, his leg *was* killing him. He had some exercises he was supposed to do at night that he hadn't done to relax the muscles. He needed to lay his leg flat in bed. He needed…he needed to know he could function as a man. The situation with Eve had been disturbing because it had never happened to him before. What if something was wrong with him? What if all those operations had done something to his libido?

You don't have any problem responding to Jewel.

He recalled his feelings for Jewel, the ones that had sent him off in search of another woman. They weren't as comforting as they should have been. He had felt the same sort of semi-arousal with Eve before he kissed her, but when it came time for action, his body had opted out.

Mac cut the pickup engine at the back door to the cottage. No lights. At least he'd be spared the ignominy of Jewel seeing him sneaking in at two in the morning. He didn't want to have to make some explanation about why he was home early. He wasn't about to tell her the truth, and he hated like hell to lie.

He eased the kitchen door open—Western doors were rarely locked, even in this day and age—and slipped inside.

"Hi."

Mac nearly lost his balance and fell. "What the hell are you doing sitting here in the dark?"

He reached for the light switch, but Jewel said, "Don't."

The rough, raw sound of her voice, as though she had been crying, stayed his hand. He remained where he was, waiting for his eyes to adjust to the dark. He finally located her in the shadows. She was sitting with her elbows perched on the kitchen table, her face buried in her hands.

He limped over, scraped a chair closer and sat beside her. He felt her stiffen as he laid an arm across her shoulder. "Are you all right?

"I'm fine."

"You don't sound fine. You sound like you've been crying."

"I didn't think you'd be back tonight."

Which meant she had expected to have the privacy to cry without being disturbed. It didn't explain *why* she had been crying. She tried to rise, but he kept his arm around her and pressed her back down. "I'm here, Jewel."

"Why is that, Mac? I can't imagine any woman throwing you out. Which means you left on your own. What happened?"

This was exactly the scene Mac had been hoping to avoid. "She...uh...we...uh..."

"Don't tell me Eve didn't make a pass."

"She did," Mac conceded reluctantly.

"Then why aren't you spending the night with her?"

"I...uh...that sort of thing can give a woman ideas."

"I see."

"You do?"

"Sure. Spend the whole night in a woman's bed, and she tends to think you might be serious about her. Everyone knows you're a love'em and leave'em kind of guy."

"I am? I mean, I suppose I am. I haven't

found a woman I'd want to settle down with who'd have me." That was certainly no lie.

Eve had wanted him, all right. It should have been the easiest thing in the world to take her in his arms and make love to her. The situation had been perfect: willing woman, intelligent, not a total stranger, attractive—hell, absolutely beautiful. And it had been absolutely impossible.

Mac bit back the sound of frustration that sought voice.

"You should go to bed if you're going to get up early and walk tomorrow," Jewel said.

"I'd rather sit here with you," Mac replied.

"I'd rather be alone."

"Are you sure?"

"I'll be fine."

Mac leaned over to kiss her softly on the temple. Her hair smelled of lilacs. It reminded him of warm, lazy summer days they had spent lying on the banks of the pond that bordered the Stonecreek Ranch. He resisted the urge to thread his fingers through her hair. It might comfort her, but it would drive him damn near crazy.

"Just know I'm here if you need me," he said. "You'd better get to bed, too, because I'm expecting you to walk with me tomorrow."

"I don't think that's a good idea. It would be better if you go alone."

He stared at her, wishing he could see the expression on her face. Moonlight filtered in through the kitchen window but left her mostly in shadow. "What's going on, Jewel? Why are you shutting me out?"

"I got along fine without you for six years, Mac. What makes you think I need you now?"

Mac was stunned as much by the virulence in her voice as by what she had said. "If you want me out of here, I'm gone."

She clutched his forearm as he rose, rubbing at her eyes with the knuckles of her other hand. "Don't leave. Don't leave."

He pulled her up and into his arms, and she grabbed him tight around his neck and sobbed against his shoulder. He rubbed her back with his open palms, aware suddenly that she was wearing a thin, sleeveless cotton nightgown and nothing else.

His body turned hard as a rock in two seconds flat.

His equipment worked all right. At the wrong time. With the wrong woman.

"Damn it all to hell," he muttered.

Jewel needed his comfort, not some male animal lusting after her. He kept their hips apart, not wanting his physical response to frighten or distress her. "Tell me what's wrong, Jewel. Let me help," he crooned in her ear.

"It's too embarrassing," she said, her face pressed tight against the curve of his shoulder.

"Nothing's too embarrassing for us to talk about, my little carbuncle."

She hiccuped a laugh. "Carbuncle? Isn't that an ugly inflammation—"

"It's a red precious stone. I swear."

She relaxed, chuckling, and it took all the willpower he had to keep from pulling her tight against him.

"You always could make me laugh," she said. "Oh, Mac, I wish you'd come back a long time ago. I missed you."

"And I missed you. Now tell me what's so embarrassing that you don't want to talk about it?"

She sighed, and her breasts swelled against his chest, soft and warm. His heartbeat picked up. Lord, she was dangerous. Why couldn't this have happened with Eve? Why did it have to be Jewel?

Her fingers began to play in the hair at his nape. He wondered if she knew what she was doing to him and decided she couldn't possibly. She wouldn't purposely turn him on. What she wanted was comfort from a friend. And he intended to give it to her.

But he wasn't any more able to stop his body from responding than he had been capable of making it respond. All he could do was try to ignore the part of him that was insisting he do something. He focused his attention on Jewel. She needed his help.

"Tell me what's wrong," he urged.

"I wish things were different, that's all."

"Don't we all?" he said, thinking of his own situation. "But frankly, that doesn't sound embarrassing enough to keep to yourself. What is it? Got bucked off your horse? Happens to the best of us. Broke a dish? Do it all the time. If you broke a heart I might worry, but you can always buy another dish."

She laughed. The bubbly, effervescent sound he hadn't heard for six years. He pulled her close and rocked her in his arms in the old, familiar, brotherly way.

She stiffened, and he realized what he had

done. His hips, with the hard bulge in front, were pressed tight against hers. There was no way she could mistake his condition.

"Damn, Jewel," he said, backing away from her, putting her at arm's length and gripping her hands tightly in his.

He smiled, but she didn't smile back.

When she pulled free, he let her go. "We can still talk," he said, wanting her to stay, wanting to confess the truth to her. She was still his best friend. But somehow things had changed. He couldn't tell her everything, not the most private things. Not anymore.

Maybe he had been wrong to expect her to confide in him. Maybe she felt the same awkwardness he did, the distance that had never been there before. A distance he had put there, because he saw her not just as a friend, but as a woman he wanted to kiss and touch.

"I'm going to bed, Mac."

"Will you walk with me tomorrow?"

"I don't think—"

"Please, Jewel. You're my best friend. I'd really like the company."

She hesitated so long, he thought she was going to refuse. "All right, Mac. I suppose I owe you that much." She turned and left without another word.

He waited until her bedroom door closed before he moved, afraid that if he did, he would go after her.

He wondered what had been troubling her. He wondered what she would have done if he had lowered his head and sucked on her breasts through the thin cotton. Blood pulsed through his rock-hard body, and he swore under his breath.

Mac went to bed, but he didn't sleep. He tossed and turned, troubled by vivid erotic fantasies of himself and Jewel Whitelaw. *Their legs entangled, their bodies entwined, his tongue deep in her mouth, his shaft deep inside her. She was calling to him, calling his name.*

Mac awoke tangled in the sheets, his body hot, hard and ready, his heart racing. And all alone.

He heard Jewel calling from outside the door. "Mac. Are you awake?" She knocked twice quietly. "It's time to walk."

Mac groaned. "I'll be with you in a minute." As soon as he was decent.

From the look of Jewel at the breakfast table,

she hadn't slept any better than he had. She was wearing something even less attractive than the sweatshirt and cutoffs she had worn previously. It didn't matter. He saw her naked.

Mac shook his head to clear it. The vision of her breasts, large and luscious as peaches, and her long, slim legs wrapped around his waist, remained as vivid as ever.

"Are you all right?" Jewel asked.

"Fine. Let's go."

She chattered the whole way to the canyon, but he would have been hard-pressed to remember a word of what she had said or his own responses.

Everything was different. Something was missing. And something had been added.

He wanted their old relationship back. He was determined to quench any desire he might feel for her, so things could get back to an even footing. He figured the best way to start was to bring the subject out into the open and deal with it. On the walk back to the house, he did.

"About what happened last night... It shouldn't have happened." His comment was vague, but he knew she understood exactly what he meant when pink roses blossomed on her cheekbones.

She shrugged. "I was just a woman in a skimpy nightgown."

"Jewel, I—"

She stopped and turned to him, looking into his eyes, her gaze earnest. "Please, Mac. Can we pretend it never happened?"

He gave a relieved sigh. "That's exactly what I'd like to do. It was an accident. I never intended for it to happen. I wish I could promise it won't happen again, but—" He shot her a chagrined look. "I'll be sure you're never embarrassed again. Am I forgiven?"

"There's no need—"

"Just say yes," he said.

"Yes."

She turned abruptly and started walking again, and he followed after her.

"I'm glad that's over with," he said. "I can't afford to lose a friend as good as you, Jewel."

"And I can't afford to lose a friend like you, Mac."

Jewel's eyes were as brown and sad as a motherless calf. Mac wished she had told him why she was crying last night. He wished she had let him comfort her. If she ever gave him another chance, he was going to do it right. He wasn't going to let his hormones get in the way of their friendship.

When they got back to the house, she hurried up the back steps ahead of him. "I get the shower first!"

"We could always share," he teased. He could have bitten his tongue out. That sort of sexual innuendo had to cease.

To his relief, Jewel gave him a wide smile and said, "In your dreams, Mac! I'll try to save you a little hot water."

Then she was gone.

Mac settled on the back stoop and rubbed the calf muscles of his injured leg. It was getting easier to walk. Practice was helping. And it would get easier to treat Jewel as merely a friend. All he had needed was a little more practice at that, too.

After he had showered, Mac made a point of seeking Jewel out, determined to work on reestablishing their friendship. He found her in the barn, cleaning stalls and shoveling in new hay for the dozen or so ponies Camp LittleHawk kept available for horseback rides. "Can I help?" he said.

"There's another pitchfork over by the door. Be my guest."

Mac noticed she didn't even look up from her work. Not a very promising sign. He grabbed the pitchfork and went to work in the stall next to the one she was working in. "I thought your mom usually hired someone to do this kind of heavy labor."

"I don't have anything better to do with my time," Jewel said.

"Why not?" Mac asked. "Pretty girl like you ought to be out enjoying herself."

Jewel stuck her pitchfork into the hay and turned to stare at him. "I enjoy my work."

"I'm sure you do," he said, throwing a pitchfork of manure into the nearby wheelbarrow. "But there's a time for work and a time for play. I don't see you doing enough playing."

"I'm a grown-up woman, Mac. Playing is for kids."

"You're never too old to play, Jewel." Mac filled his pitchfork with clean straw and threw it up over the stall so it landed on Jewel's head.

She came out of her stall sputtering and picking straw out of her mouth, mad as a peeled rattler. She confronted him, hands on hips and said, "That wasn't funny!"

He set his pitchfork against the stall and laughed. "I think you look darned cute with straw sticking out of your hair every which-away." He headed toward her to help pull out some of the straw.

When he got close enough, she gave him a shove that sent him onto his behind. Only the straw Mac landed in wasn't clean. He gave a howl of outrage and struggled up out of the muck, glaring at the stain on the back of his jeans. "What'd you do that for?"

She grinned. "I think you look darned cute, all covered with muck."

"You know this means war."

"No, Mac. We're even now. Don't—"

He lunged toward her, caught her by the waist and threw her up over his shoulder in a fireman's carry.

"Watch out for your leg!" Jewel cried. "You're going to hurt yourself carrying me like this."

"My leg is fine," Mac growled. "Good enough to get you where I want you."

Mac headed for the short stack of hay at one end of the barn and when he got there, dropped Jewel into it. When she tried to jump free, he came down on top of her and pinned her hands on either side of her.

"Mac," she said breathlessly, laughing. "Get up."

"I want to play some more, Emerald, my dear," he said sprinkling her hair with hay.

"You're more green than I am," she taunted.

Mac took a look at the back of his jeans. "Yes, and I think you should pay a forfeit for that."

"You can have the shower first," she said with a bubbly laugh. "You need it!"

His laugh was cut off when he realized that what he really wanted was a kiss. He stared at her curving mouth, at the way her nose wrinkled when she laughed, at the teasing sparkle in her brown eyes. "I think I'll take something now."

He watched her face sober when she realized what he intended. He knew she must be able to feel his arousal, cradled as he was between her jean-clad thighs. He waited for her to tell him to let go, that the game was over. She stared up at him with luminous eyes and slicked her tongue quickly, nervously over her lips. But she didn't say get up or get off. And she didn't say no.

Friends, Mac. Not lovers. Friends.

Mac made himself kiss her eyelids closed before he kissed each cheek and then her nose and then...her forehead.

He rose abruptly and pulled her to her feet. She was dizzy, because her eyes had been closed, so he was forced to hold her in his arms until she was steady. She felt so good there, so very right. And so very wrong.

"I'm sorry, Jewel," he said. "That was totally out of line."

She took a deep breath and let it out. "Yes, I suppose it was. I think it's your turn to pay a forfeit, Mac."

He tensed. "What did you have in mind?"

She reached out, and for a moment he thought she was going to lay her hand on his chest and give him another shove. Instead, she grasped a nearby pitchfork and held it out to him. "You get to finish what I started. I'm going to get another shower and wash off all this itchy straw."

"Hey! That's not fair," he protested.

But she had already turned and stalked away.

"You and your bright ideas," Mac muttered

to himself as he pitched manure into the wheel-barrow. "What were you thinking? Maybe you could throw straw around when you were kids and it was funny, but there was nothing funny about what almost happened in that haystack. What if you'd kissed her lips? How would you have felt when she got upset?

How do you know she'd have been upset?

Mac mused over that question for the next hour as he finished cleaning stalls. Actually, Jewel had seemed more upset that he hadn't kissed her lips. Could she have feelings for him that weren't merely friendly?

Don't even think about it, Macready. The woman's off-limits. She's your friend, and she needs your friendship. Concentrate on somebody else's needs for a change and forget what you want.

Mac knew why he was having all these lurid thoughts about Jewel. He probably would be having such thoughts about any woman he came in close contact with at this stage in his life. It didn't help that Jewel turned him on so hard and fast.

Get over it, Mac.

"I intend to," Mac muttered as he set the

pitchfork back where it belonged and headed for the house. "Jewel is my friend. And that's the way it's going to stay."

At the end of two weeks Mac was walking the mile to the canyon without the aid of a cane and doing it in seven minutes flat. Jewel had difficulty keeping up with him when he broke into a jog. His leg was getting better; hers never would. She could picture him moving away from her, going on with his life, leaving her behind. She was going to miss him. She was going to miss playing with him.

The scene in the barn hadn't been repeated. Nor had Mac teased her or taunted her or done any of the playful things he might have done when they were teenagers. He had become a serious grown-up over the past two weeks. She hadn't realized how much she had needed him to play with her. To her surprise, she hadn't been intimidated or frightened by him in the barn. Not even when she had thought he might kiss her.

She had wanted that kiss, she realized, and been sorely disappointed when he kissed her forehead instead. Then she'd realized he had been carried away by their physical closeness, and when he'd realized it was her—his old friend, Jewel—he had backed off. He liked her, but not that way. They were just friends.

It should have been enough. But lately, Jewel was realizing she wanted more. She was going to have to control those feelings, or she would ruin everything. Mac would be leaving soon enough. She didn't want to drive him away by asking for things from him he wasn't willing to give.

"Hey," she called ahead to him. "How about taking a break at the bottom of the canyon."

"You got it." He dropped onto the warm, sandy ground with his back against the stone wall that bore the primitive Native American drawings and sifted the soil through his fingers. She sank down across from him, leaning back on her palms, her legs in front of her.

"You'll be running full out by this time next week," she said.

"I expect so."

"I won't be coming with you then."

"Why not?"

She sat up and rubbed at the sore muscles in her thigh. "I can't keep up with you, Mac." In more ways than one. He would be going places, while she stayed behind.

Mac dusted off his hands on his shorts, scooted around to her side and, as though it were the most natural thing in the world, began to massage her thigh. She hadn't let a man touch her like that since she had broken her engagement. Chill bumps rose on her skin at the feel of Mac's callused fingers on her flesh. It felt amazingly good. It dawned on her that she didn't feel the least bit afraid. But then, this was Mac. He would never hurt her.

The past two weeks of waiting for Mac to repeat his behavior in the barn had been wonderful and horrible. She loved being with Mac. And she dreaded it. Since the night he had come home early from Evelyn Latham's house, he had remained an avuncular friend. He had been a tremendous help planning activities for the children. He had made her laugh often. But with the exception of that brief, unfulfilled promise in the barn, there was nothing the least bit sexual in his behavior toward her.

She was unsure of what her feelings were for Mac, but there was no doubting her profound physical reaction to his touch. It was difficult not to look at him as a virile, attractive man, rather than merely as a friend. Even now, she couldn't keep her eyes off of him.

The Texas sun had turned him a warm bronze, but a white strip of flesh showed around the waist of his running shorts, confirming the hidden skin was lighter. She caught herself wondering what he would look like without the shorts.

"How does that feel?" he asked as he massaged her thigh. "Better?"

She nodded because she couldn't speak. *It feels wonderful.* She wanted his hands to move higher, between her legs. As though she had willed it, his fingertips moved upward on her thigh. She let him keep up the massage, because it felt good. Then stopped him because it felt too good.

"Wait." She gripped his wrist with her hand, afraid that he would read her mind and realize that the last thing she wanted him to do was stop.

"If you exercised more, maybe your limp wouldn't be so bad," he said.

She brushed his hand away from where it lingered on her flesh. "One leg is slightly shorter than the other, Mac. That isn't going to change with exercise.''

"It might with surgery. They can do remarkable things these days. Have you thought about—''

"What's going on here, Mac?'' she interrupted. "You never said a word to me in the past about my limp. You always told me to ignore it, to pretend it didn't exist, that it didn't keep me from being who I am. What's changed?''

Mac backed up against the wall again. His gaze was concentrated on the sand he began once more sifting through his fingers.

"Mac?'' she persisted. "Answer me.''

He looked up at her, his eyes searching her face. "How can you stand it—not being able to run?''

She shrugged. "I manage.''

"I'd hate it if something like that happened to me.''

"Something like that *has* happened to you.''

He shook his head. "Uh-uh. I'm temporarily out of commission. I'm going to be as good as new.''

Did he really believe that? Jewel wondered.

Yes, he had made astonishing progress in two weeks, but even she could see the effort it had taken. One look at his leg—at the scar tissue on his leg—suggested there was never going to be as much muscle to work with as there had been in the past. "What if you can never run again like you used to, Mac? What if you can't get back to where you were?"

"I will."

"What if you can't?"

"I'll be playing again in the fall. Count on it."

"You're purposely avoiding my question. *What if you can't?*"

He rose, but it took obvious effort to do so without the cane. She said nothing while he accomplished the feat—a minor miracle considering the condition he'd been in two weeks ago.

"Let's go," he said gruffly, reaching down to help her to her feet.

She shoved his hand out of the way. "I'm not a cripple, either, Mac," she said. "I can manage on my own."

"Damn it, Jewel! What do you want from me?"

"Honesty," she said, rising and standing toe

to toe with him, her eyes focused on his. "You never used to lie to me, Mac. Or to yourself."

"What is it you want to hear me say? I won't quit playing football! It's all I ever wanted to do."

"You wanted to be a paleontologist."

"That's what I said. But inside—" he thumped his bare chest with his fist "—all I ever dreamed about, all I ever wanted to do was run like the wind and catch footballs. It was just so impossible for so long, I never let myself hope for it too much. But I made it happen. And I'm not going to give it up!"

Jewel felt her heart skip a beat. She hadn't known. She hadn't realized. If what Mac said was true, then he was facing a much greater crisis than she had imagined.

"Avoiding reality isn't going to make it go away, Mac," she said gently. "You have to face your demons."

"Like you have?" Mac retorted.

Jewel's face blanched. She turned her back on him and headed up the trail toward the mouth of the canyon.

"Jewel, wait," Mac said as he hurried after her. He grabbed her arm to stop her. "If you're going to insist on honesty from me, how about a little from you?''

''What is it you want to know? You know everything,'' she said bitterly. ''You're the only one who does!''

He gave her an incredulous look. ''You never told anyone else? What about your fiancé?''

She shook her head violently.

''Why the hell not?''

''I couldn't tell Jerry. I just couldn't!''

In days gone by he would have put an arm around her to offer her comfort. But things had changed somehow in the two weeks since they had met again. His eyes offered emotional support, instead. ''God, Jewel. That's a heavy burden to be carrying around all by yourself.''

''I'm managing all right.''

''What happened to Jerry What's-his-name? Why did you call off the wedding?''

''I couldn't... I wasn't able... I could never...''

She saw the dawning comprehension in his eyes. ''I don't want or need your pity!'' She tried to run from him in awkward, hobbling strides, but he quickly caught up to her and pulled her into his arms.

''Don't run away,'' he said, his arms closing

tightly around her. "It doesn't matter, Jewel. It'll get better with time."

She made a keening sound in her throat. "It's been six years. I can't forget what happened, Mac. I can't get it out of my head. Jerry was so patient, but when he tried to make love to me, I couldn't let him do it. I couldn't!" Her throat ached. A hot tear spilled onto her cheek and a sob broke free.

She grasped Mac tight around the waist and pressed her face against his bare chest, sobbing as she never had on the day she had been attacked or at any time since then. She had been too numb with shock to cry six years ago. And she had been too full of guilt when she broke up with Jerry to allow herself the release of tears.

"Shh. Shh," Mac crooned as he rocked her in his arms. "It's all right. It doesn't matter. Everything will be all right."

She felt his lips against her hair, soothing, comforting, and then his hands on either side of her face as he raised it to kiss her tear-wet eyelids. He kissed her nose and her cheeks and finally her mouth. His lips were firm, yet gentle, against her own. She yielded to the insistent pressure of his mouth, her lips soft and damp beneath his. He kissed her again, his lips brushing across hers and sending a surprising frisson of desire skittering down her spine. *Oh, Mac...*

She pressed her lips back against his and heard a sharp intake of breath. She froze, then stepped back and stared up at him in confusion.

He opened his mouth to speak and shut it again, obviously upset and looking for a way to explain what had happened between them. She wondered if he had felt it, too, the wondrous stirring inside, the need to merge into one another. What if he did? Oh, God. It would ruin everything. She couldn't...and he would never... She took another step back from him.

"Wait, Jewel. Don't go," he said, reaching out a hand to her. "We have to talk about this."

"What is there to say?"

He took a step closer, and it took all her willpower not to run from him. She felt an equally driving need to press herself against him, which she resisted just as fiercely.

"I don't want what just happened to spoil things between us," he said, his voice anguished. "I could see you needed comfort, and I...I got a little carried away."

"All right, Mac. If that's the way you want it." She would ruin everything if she pressed for more. He obviously wanted things to stay the same between them. He wanted them to be friends. That was probably for the best. What if she tried loving him and failed, as she had with Jerry? She would lose everything. She couldn't bear that.

"What's wrong, Jewel?"

She mentally and physically squared her shoulders. "I shouldn't have fallen apart like that. I've spent a lot of time in counseling putting what happened six years ago behind me."

"Have you?"

"I'm as over it as I'm ever going to get," she conceded with a rueful twist of her mouth. "It doesn't matter, Mac, really. I have the kids at camp. I have friends. I have a full life."

"Without a man in it," he said flatly. "Or children."

She arched a brow. "Who says a woman needs a man in her life? And there are lots of children at Camp LittleHawk who need me."

He held up his hands in surrender. "You win. I'm not going to argue the point."

Jewel released a breath that became a sigh, glad the subject was closed. "We'd better get back to the house."

He looked as though he wanted to continue the discussion, but she knew that wouldn't help the situation. She decided levity was what was needed. "I hope you saved some energy, because I know for a fact Colt will be waiting for you when you get back to the house.''

Mac groaned. ''I forgot. He's going to throw me some passes.''

''I can always send him away.''

''I suppose I can catch a few passes and keep him happy.''

''And keep who happy?''

Mac grinned. ''So I'm looking forward to it. Think what that'll mean to you.''

She gave him a quizzical look. If Mac was up to catching passes, it meant he was getting well. If he was getting well, it meant he would be leaving soon. She wanted to hear him say it. Maybe then she could stop fantasizing about him. ''What will it mean to me?'' she asked.

Twin dimples appeared in his cheeks. ''You get the shower first.''

Jewel laughed. It beat the heck out of crying.

Chapter 5

If there was one thing Colt Whitelaw wanted more than he wanted to fly jets someday, it was to have Jennifer Wright look at him the way she looked at his best friend, Huckleberry Duncan. Jenny didn't even care that Huck had a stupid name. When Huck was around, Jenny wouldn't have noticed if Colt dropped dead at her feet. She only had eyes for Huck.

Which meant Colt got to spend a lot of time watching her when she wasn't looking. Jenny wasn't what most guys would have called pretty. She was short and skinny, her nose was too long and her teeth were slightly crooked. But she had the prettiest eyes he'd ever seen. Jenny's eyes were about the bluest blue eyes could get.

It wasn't just the color of them that he found attractive. When he looked into Jenny's eyes he saw the pledge of warmth, the promise of humor and depths of wisdom far beyond what a four-teen-year-old girl ought to possess.

Jenny might be the same age as him and Huck, but it seemed she had grown up faster—in more ways than one. For a couple of years she'd been taller than Huck. This past year Huck had caught up and passed her. Colt had always been taller than Jenny. Not that she'd noticed.

This past year something else had happened to Jenny. She had started becoming a woman. Colt felt like walloping Huck when Huck kidded her about the bumps she was sprouting up front, but when she bent over laughing and her shirt fell away, he had sneaked a peek at them. They were pure white and pink-tipped. He had turned away pretty quick because the whole time he was looking, he couldn't seem to breathe.

His body did strange things these days when-ever she was around. His stomach turned upside down and his heart started to race and his body embarrassed him by doing other things that were still pretty new and felt amazingly good and grown-up. He had it bad for Jenny Wright. Not that he'd ever let her or Huck know about it. Because Huck felt about Jenny the way Jenny felt about Huck. It was true love both ways. When they got old enough, Colt figured they'd marry for sure.

He kept his feelings to himself. He liked Huck too much to give him up as a friend. And it would have killed him to stop seeing Jenny. Even if she was always going to be Huck's girl.

"Hey, Colt. I thought you were going to throw me some passes," Huck said, giving him a friendly chuck on the shoulder.

Colt watched as Jenny climbed up onto the top rail of the corral near the new counselors' cottages and shoved her long blond ponytail back over her shoulder. "You gonna be all right up there?" he asked.

She laughed. "I'm not one of your mom's campers, Colt. I'm healthy as a horse. I'll be fine."

Colt couldn't help it if he worried about her. He didn't want her to fall and get hurt. Not that she appreciated his concern. He turned the football in his hands, finding the laces and placing his hands where he knew they needed to be.

"Go long!" he shouted to Huck, who had already started to run over the uneven terrain, which was dotted with clumps of buffalo grass and an occasional prickly pear cactus.

Colt threw the ball with ease and watched it fall perfectly, gently into Huck's outstretched hands. Huck did a victory dance and spiked the ball.

"We are the greatest!" Huck shouted, holding his pointed fingers upward on either side of him in the referee's signal for a touchdown.

They made a pretty good team, Colt conceded. About the best in the state. Both of them would likely be offered athletic scholarships to college. Huck was so rich—his father was a U.S. senator from Texas—he didn't need a scholarship to pay for college. Colt's family could easily afford to send him to college, too, but he kept playing football because he had heard it might help him get into the Air Force Academy.

If Huck had wanted to go to the Academy, his dad, the senator, could write a letter and get him appointed. Colt didn't have that advantage. He would never presume on his friendship with Huck to ask for that kind of favor from Senator Duncan. So he had to find another way to make sure he got in.

Huck retrieved the ball and started walking back toward Colt and Jenny. Colt took advantage of the opportunity to have Jenny's full attention. "He's pretty good," he said, knowing Huck was the one thing Jenny was always willing to discuss.

"He is, isn't he," she said, a worried frown forming between her brows.

"Something wrong with that?" Colt asked, leaning his elbow casually on the top rail next to Jenny's thigh where her cutoffs ended and her flesh began. Casual. Right. His mouth was bone-dry.

"I don't want him to go away," she said.

He watched her face as she watched Huck. "You think football will take him away?"

"No. Huck loves football, but I think he'd be willing to attend a college somewhere close just so we could be together. Only..." Her head swiveled suddenly, and she looked him right in the eye. "You're going to take him away."

He swallowed hard, his hormones going into overdrive as she continued staring at him. He managed to say, "I am?"

She nodded solemnly. "He's going to want to follow wherever you go, Colt, and I know your plans don't include staying here in Texas. I don't want to get left behind.''

Jenny was dirt-poor, and even if she could have gotten a scholarship to a college somewhere else—which, with her brains, she probably could—she had to stay at the Double D Ranch to help take care of her sick mother and four younger brothers.

''Huck would never leave you behind,'' Colt said seriously.

''He might not have any choice. Not if he went off to fly jets somewhere with you.''

Colt felt angry, vulnerable and exposed. ''How did you know about that? About me wanting to fly jets?''

She shrugged and slipped down off the top rail of the corral. ''Huck and I don't have any secrets.''

''He shouldn't have told you,'' Colt said, feeling his heart begin to thud at the closeness of her. He wanted her to step back so he could breathe, so he could think straight. Didn't she see what she was doing to him? ''That was private information,'' he snapped. ''It doesn't concern you.''

Her fisted hands found her hips. ''It does when Huck is thinking about going with you.''

"I never asked him to come along," he retorted.

"Hey, you two! What're my two favorite people arguing about?" Huck said, grinning as he stepped between them and slipped an arm around each of their shoulders. Colt stood rigid beneath his arm. Huck still had the football in one hand, and Colt knocked it to the ground.

"Ask your girlfriend," he said, bending to retrieve the ball and pulling free of Huck's arm. "I've got to go find Mac Macready. I'm supposed to throw some passes to him this morning."

Huck left Jenny standing where she was and headed after Colt. "Macready's really here? I mean, I heard rumors in town he was, but I wasn't sure. You're really going to throw some balls to him?"

"I said I was, didn't I?" Colt stopped where he was and looked back over Huck's shoulder to where Jenny stood abandoned. Her expression said it all.

See what I mean? You lead. Huck follows.

It wasn't his fault. It had always been that way. If Jenny didn't like it, she didn't have to hang around. Colt turned back to Huck.

Huck's sandy hair had fallen over his brow

and into his eyes. His rarely combed hair, combined with his ski-slope nose and freckled cheeks and broad smile, gave him an affable appearance he deserved. Huck didn't make enemies. He wouldn't have hurt a fly. Colt was sure he hadn't meant to hurt Jenny's feelings. Huck just forgot to be thoughtful sometimes.

"What about Jenny?" Colt asked.

"Hey, Jenny," Huck called. "You want to hang around and meet Mac Macready?"

Jenny shook her head.

"See? She's not interested," Huck said. "But I am."

Colt sighed. "You want to stay?" he asked Huck.

"Does a cowboy wear spurs?" Huck replied with a lopsided grin.

They headed for the counselor's cottage where Mac was staying, leaving Jenny behind at the corral. Colt glanced over his shoulder at her. It looked for a moment like she might follow them. Then she turned to where her horse was tied to the corral next to Huck's, mounted up and loped the gelding in the direction of her family's ranch.

"You shouldn't ignore Jenny like that," Colt said, turning back to Huck.

Huck seemed to notice suddenly that she had left. "What did I do?" He shook his head. "Women. They're mysterious creatures, old buddy. Don't ever try to understand them. It's a waste of time."

"Why did you tell her about me wanting to fly?" Colt asked.

Huck looked chagrined. "We were talking about the future and...it just came up."

"Make sure it doesn't come up again," Colt said. "That's my business, and I don't want the whole world knowing about it." Especially when he was afraid he wasn't going to be able to make his dream come true.

"Jenny isn't the whole world," Huck argued. "She's my girlfriend. I have to tell her things."

"Just don't tell her things about me," Colt insisted.

"That's hard to avoid when you're my best friend," Huck said. "Besides, if we're going to be jet pilots—"

"When did my plans become yours?" Colt asked.

Huck grinned and pulled an arm tight around Colt's neck in a wrestler's hold. "We're friends forever, pal. Where you go, I go. If you fly, I fly. Enough said?"

Colt wished it were that simple. He wished he could express his desire to be a jet fighter pilot and expect his parents to be happy about it. He had never said a word to them, because he knew they would hate the idea.

He might be one of eight adopted kids, but his mom and dad had made it pretty clear over the past couple of years that he was the one they expected to inherit Hawk's Pride. They already had his life planned for him. They expected him to come back home after college to manage the ranch.

He was grateful to have Zach and Rebecca Whitelaw for parents. He loved them enough to want to make them happy by fulfilling their expectations. It just wasn't what he wanted for himself. He wanted to fly.

So he made his plans surreptitiously, meanwhile letting his father teach him everything he would need to know to run the cattle and quarter horse end of the business. His father had told him his sister Jewel was taking over Camp LittleHawk, and that was fine with him. Although he kind of liked the ranching business, he wanted absolutely nothing to do with a camp for kids with cancer.

Not that he didn't have sympathy for the

plight of all those sick kids. But he had learned his lesson early. He had befriended a couple of them when he was old enough to make friends. It was only later, when he asked why they hadn't returned the following summer, that he learned the awful truth. Sometimes sick people died.

It was a sobering lesson: *Illness could rob you of people you loved.* He had found a child's solution to the problem that had stood him in good stead. He stayed away from sick people. Which was why he hadn't been to Jenny's house much, even though Huck went there a lot. Her mom was dying slowly but surely of breast cancer.

Colt might have argued further with Huck, except he caught sight of Mac Macready coming around the corner of the house with his sister, Jewel.

"Hey!" Colt called. "Ready to catch a few passes?"

"You bet," Mac called back.

Colt looked for signs of reluctance or resignation on Mac's face. After all, Colt was just a kid. He didn't see anything but delight.

"Just give me a minute," Mac said with a smile and a wave. "Be right with you." He turned and said something in Jewel's ear, then headed in Colt's direction.

* * *

Jewel heard the kitchen screen door open and called, "Is that you, Mac?"

"Jewel?"

"Colt?" At the sound of her brother's frightened voice, Jewel hurried from her bedroom wearing an oversized plaid Western shirt, jeans and boots, her hair still wet from her shower. She met Colt halfway to the kitchen. "What's wrong?"

Her brother stood white-faced before her. "It's Mac. He fell."

Oh, dear God. "Should I call an ambulance?"

"I don't know," Colt said, his hands visibly trembling. "I thought maybe you ought to come and see for yourself first. It was awful, Jewel. One minute Mac was fine, and then Huck tackled him and...he didn't get up."

"Huck *tackled* him? What on earth were you boys thinking, Colt? You know Mac's recovering from surgery!"

"We thought it would be more fun—"

"Did he hit his head when he fell?"

"I don't think so. I think—"

Before Jewel could make the decision whether to call 911, Mac appeared at the kitchen door, one arm around Huck's shoulder, the other pressed against the thigh of his scarred leg.

Colt had been pale, but Mac's face was completely drained of blood. His teeth were gritted against the pain, and he was leaning heavily on Huck Duncan's shoulder and favoring his leg. It took her a second to realize it wasn't his poor, wounded and scarred left leg he was favoring, it was the other one. Now both legs were injured!

"What happened?" she asked as she crossed quickly to hold the screen door open for him. As soon as she moved, Colt seemed to wake from his shocked trance and took a place on Mac's other side. The two boys helped him keep his weight off both legs as they eased him through the kitchen and onto the sofa in the living room.

While the boys stood awkwardly at her side, Jewel dropped to her knees and eased Mac's foot up onto a rawhide stool that Grandpa Garth had given her one Christmas, a relic of bygone days at his ranch, Hawk's Way. Then she started untying the laces of Mac's athletic shoe.

"I can do that," he said, trying to brush her hands away.

"Sure you can, but let me," she insisted. She eased off the shoe and the sock beneath it and immediately saw the problem. His ankle was swelling. "Can you move it?" she asked.

Slowly, hissing in a breath, he rotated the ankle. "Doesn't feel broken," he said. "I've had enough sprains to recognize one when I see it. Damn. This is all I needed."

"I'm sorry, Mr. Macready," Huck said in an anguished voice. "I didn't mean to hurt you."

Mac looked up at the boy and said, "Call me Mac. And it wasn't your fault, Huck. Your tackle wasn't what caused the problem. I just didn't see that gopher hole soon enough."

Jewel watched him smile at the boy, pretending it was no big deal, when she knew very well it was. This was a setback, no doubt about it.

"But your leg—" Huck protested, his eyes skipping from the awful scars on Mac's left leg to the swelling on his right ankle. "How're you gonna walk now?"

"One step at a time," Mac quipped with an easy grin. "Fortunately, I brought a cane with me. That should help matters some."

Jewel turned to Colt and said, "Wrap some ice in a towel and bring it here. You go help him, Huck."

When they were both gone, she gently moved the ankle. "Are you sure it isn't broken?"

He sighed. It was a sound of disgust. "It's a sprain, Jewel. Not even a bad one."

"I should have warned you about gopher holes," she said.

"I didn't step in a gopher hole," he said quietly, looking at the hands he held fisted against his thighs.

"Then what—" She saw the truth in the wary look he gave her. His leg—his *right* leg—must not have supported him. She reached out a hand, and he clutched it with one of his.

She didn't offer him words of comfort. She could see from the grim look on his face that words wouldn't change what had happened. She didn't point out the obvious—that his football career was over. He had to see that for himself.

But if she had thought this accident would make Mac quit, he quickly disabused her of the notion.

"This'll slow down my rehabilitation some," he said. "Will you mind if I hang around a little longer? I know camp's starting in a day or so—"

She rose to her feet, her hand coming free of his. "Of course you can stay!" she said, her voice unnaturally sharp. She didn't want him to go away. She liked having him here. But she couldn't believe he was ignoring the implications of this injury. How long was he going to go on batting his head against the wall? Couldn't he see the truth? Didn't he understand what this accident meant?

"Mac—"

He cut her off with a shake of his head. "Don't say it. Don't even suggest it."

"Suggest what?"

"This doesn't change my plans."

"But—"

His face turned hard, jaw jutting, shoulders braced in determination. She had seen that look before, but she had been too young and naive to recognize it for what it was.

"Be my friend, Jewel," he said. "Don't tell me why I can't do what I want to do. Just help me to do it."

She stared at him as though she had never seen him before. She knew now why Peter Macready had survived a form of cancer that killed most kids. Why he had become the best rookie receiver in the NFL, despite the fact he had never been the fastest athlete on the field. Mac didn't give up. Mac didn't see obstacles. He saw his goal and headed for it without worrying about whether it could be reached. And so he invariably reached it.

Jewel wished she had half his confidence. She might be a married woman now with a baby in her arms.

Maybe it wasn't too late for her. Maybe she could learn from him how it was done. Maybe she could take advantage of Mac's presence to give her the impetus to change her life. If Mac could recover from a shattered leg, why couldn't she recover from a shattered life?

The boys returned with two dish towels loaded with ice and fell all over each other arranging the cold compresses around Mac's ankle. Jewel saw Mac wince when their overenthusiasm rocked his ankle, but instead of snapping at them, he launched into a story about how he had played a whole football game with a taped-up sprained ankle, thanks to an injection of painkiller.

The teenage boys dropped to his feet in awe and admiration. Jewel started to leave, but Mac reached up and caught her hand. "Join us," he said.

"I have work—"

"Just for a few minutes."

She figured maybe he didn't want to be stuck

alone with the boys. She would stay with him long enough to let them hear a story or two before shooing them away. She settled beside Mac on the worn leather couch—another donation from her grandfather's house at Hawk's Way. Mac's arm slid around her as naturally as if he did it every day.

She resisted the urge to lay her head on his shoulder. Putting his arm around her had been a friendly gesture, nothing more. But she was aware of the way his hand cupped her shoulder, massaging it as he regaled the three of them with stories of life in the pro football arena.

As she sat listening to him, an insidious idea took root.

What if she came to Mac tonight and explained her problem and asked him to help her out?

She trusted Mac not to hurt her. She trusted him to go slow, to be patient. He didn't love her, and she didn't love him, so there wouldn't be that particular pitfall complicating matters. It would be just one friend helping out another.

She could even explain to him how she had gotten the idea. That she had seen his determination to play football again and been inspired to try to solve a problem that she had thought would never be resolved.

All she wanted him to do was teach her how to arouse a man and satisfy him...and be satisfied by him.

She tried to imagine how Mac might react to such a suggestion. He was obviously an experienced man of the world. Only... What if he wasn't attracted to her that way?

Her mind flashed back to the scene in the canyon earlier that afternoon, when she had felt Mac's arousal. But he had apologized for that. Maybe when push came to shove, he wouldn't want to get involved with her.

Jewel didn't hear much of what Mac said to Colt and Huck. She wasn't even aware when he sent them away. She was lost deep in her own thoughts. And fears.

She wished the idea hadn't come to her so early in the day. Now she would be stuck thinking about it until dark, worrying it like a dog worried a bone.

All she had to do was cross the hall tonight and knock on Mac's door and... She didn't let her imagination take her any farther than that. Oh, how she wished night were here already! It was so much easier to act on impulse than to do something like this with cold calculation.

Of course, she was far from cold when she thought about Mac. Her whole body felt warm at the thought of having him touch her, having him kiss and caress her. She just wanted to get through the entire sexual act once without cringing or falling apart. That's all she wanted Mac to do for her. Just get her through the moments of panic before he did it. Get in and get out, like a quick lube job on the truck.

The absurdity of that comparison made her chuckle.

"Are you going to let me in on the joke?" Mac said.

"Maybe." If she didn't lose her nerve before nightfall.

Chapter 6

Mac was lying in bed wondering what Jewel would do if he crossed the hall, knocked on her door and told her he wanted to make love to her. She would probably think he had lost his mind. He had to resist the urge to pursue her. Jewel didn't need a fumbling, first-time lover. He, of all people, knew how much she needed a kind, considerate, *knowledgeable* bed partner. Which, of course, he wasn't.

She needed a slow hand, an easy touch—wasn't that what the song said? He had a lot of pent-up passion, a lot of celibate years to make up for. He was afraid the first time for him was going to be fast and hard. Which might be fine for him. But not for her.

Mac wished he didn't have such vivid memories of what had happened to Jewel that day in July six years ago. Any man who had seen her after Harvey Barnes had attacked her… He made himself think the word. After Harvey Barnes had *raped* her…

He had never wanted to kill a man before or since. He had been there to come to her rescue because he had seen Harvey drinking too much and worried about her, like a brother might worry about his sister. Jewel would have pounded him flat if she'd known he had followed her and Harvey when they slipped off into the trees down by the river.

He had kept his distance, even considered turning around and heading back to the noise of the carnival rides at the picnic, which seemed a world away from the soothing rustle of leaves down by the river. He had heard her laugh and then…silence.

He figured Harvey must be kissing her. He was standing at the edge of the river skipping stones, thinking he'd been an idiot to follow her, when he heard her cry out. Even then, he hadn't been sure at first whether it was a cry of passion.

The second cry had chilled his blood and started him running toward the sound. He could remember the feeling of terror as he searched frantically for her amid the thick laurel bushes and the tangle of wild ivy at the river's edge, calling her name and getting no answer.

There were no more cries. He saw why when he finally found them. Harvey had his hand pressed tight over Jewel's mouth, and she was struggling vainly beneath him. He saw something white on the ground nearby and realized it was her underpants.

He might have killed Harvey, if Jewel hadn't stopped him. He hadn't even been aware of his hands clenched in the flesh at Harvey's throat. It was only Jewel's anguished voice in his ear, pleading with him, that made him stop before he strangled the life out of the boy.

Harvey was nearly unconscious by the time Mac finally let go and turned to Jewel. Seeing her torn, grass-stained dress and the trickle of blood coming from her lip enraged him all over again. Jewel whimpered with fear—of him, he realized suddenly—and the fight went out of him.

He started toward her to hold her, to comfort her, but she clutched her arms tight around herself, turned her back to him and cried, "Don't touch me! Don't look at me!"

His heart was thudding loudly in his chest. "Jewel," he said. "You need to go to the hospital. Let me find your parents—"

She whirled on him and rasped, "No! Please don't tell anybody."

"But you're hurt!"

"My father will kill him," she whispered.

He could understand that. He had almost killed Harvey Barnes himself. Then she gave the reason that persuaded him to keep his silence.

"Everyone will know," she said, her brown eyes stark. "I couldn't bear it, Mac. Please. Help me."

"We'll have to say something to explain that cut on your lip," he said tersely. "And the grass stains on your dress."

"My beautiful dress." The tears welled in her eyes as she pulled the skirt around to look at the grass stains on the back of it.

He realized it wasn't the dress she was crying for, but the other beautiful thing she had lost. Her innocence.

"We'll tell your father Harvey attacked you—"

"No. Please!"

He reached out to take her shoulders, and she shrank from him. His hands dropped to his sides. He realized they were trembling and curled them into tight fists. "We'll tell them Harvey attacked you, but you fought him off," he said in an urgent voice. "Unless you tell that much of the tale, they're liable to believe the worst."

He had never seen—never hoped to see again—a look as desolate as the one she gave him.

"All right," she said. "But tell them you came in time. Tell them...nothing happened."

"What if...what if you're pregnant?" he asked.

"I don't think...I don't think..."

He realized she was in too much shock to even contemplate the possibility.

She shook her head, looking dazed and confused. "I don't think..."

He thought concealing the truth was a bad idea. She needed medical attention. She needed the comfort her mother and father could give her. "Jewel, let me tell your parents," he pleaded quietly.

She shook her head and began to shiver.

"Give me your hand, Jewel," he said, afraid to put his arms around her, afraid she might scream or faint or something equally terrifying.

She kept her arms wrapped around herself and started walking in the opposite direction from the revelers at the picnic. "Take me home, Mac," she said. "Please, just take me home."

He snatched up her underpants, stuffed them in his Levi's pocket and followed her to his truck. But it was too much to hope they would escape unnoticed. Not with Jewel's seven brothers and sisters at the picnic.

It was Rolleen who caught them before they could escape. She insisted Mac find her parents, and he'd had no choice except to go hunting for Zach and Rebecca. He had found Zach first.

The older man's eyes had turned flinty as he listened to Mac's abbreviated—and edited—version of what had happened.

The dangerous, animal sound that erupted from Zach's throat when he saw Jewel's torn dress and her bruised face and swollen lip made Mac's neck hairs stand upright. He realized suddenly that Jewel had known her father better than he had. Zach became a lethal predator. Only the lack of a quarry contained his killing rage.

Jewel's family surrounded her protectively, unconsciously shutting him out. He was forced to stand aside as they led her away. It wasn't until he got back to his private room in the cottage he shared with a half-dozen boys aged eight to twelve and stripped off his jeans, that he realized he still had Jewel's underwear in his pocket.

The garment was white cotton, with a delicate lace trim. It was stained with blood.

A painful lump rose in his throat, and his eyes burned with tears he was too grown up to shed. He fought the sobs that bunched like a fist in his chest, afraid one of the campers would return and hear him through the wall that separated his room from theirs. He pressed his mouth against a pillow in the bedroom and held it there until the ache eased, and he thought the danger was over.

In the shower later, where no one could see or hear, he shed tears of frustration and rage and despair. He had known, even then, that Harvey Barnes had stolen something precious from him that day, as well.

Mac learned later that Zach had found Harvey Barnes and horsewhipped him within an inch of his life. And Zach hadn't even known the full extent of Harvey's crime against his daughter. It seemed Jewel had been right not to tell her father the truth. Zach would have killed the boy for sure. Harvey's parents had sent him away, and he hadn't been seen since.

Things weren't the same between him and Jewel after that. She smiled and pretended everything was all right in front of him and her family. But the smile on her lips never reached her eyes.

The end of the summer came too soon, before they had reconciled their friendship. He went to her the night before he left, seeking somehow to mend the breach between them, to say goodbye for the summer and to ask if she was all right.

"Harvey Barnes is gone," she said. "And tomorrow you will be, too. Then I can forget about what happened."

"I'll be back next year," he reminded her.

She had been looking at her knotted hands when she said, "I hope you won't come, Mac."

Something bunched up tight inside of him. "Not come? I come every summer, Jewel."

"Don't come back. As a favor to me, Mac. Please don't come back."

"But why? You're my best friend, Jewel. I—"

"You know," she said in a brittle voice. She raised her eyes and looked at him and let him see her pain. "You know the truth. It's in your eyes every time you look at me."

He felt like crying again and forced himself to swallow back the tickle in his throat. "Jewel—"

"I want to forget, Mac," she said. "I need to forget. Please, please don't come back."

A lump of grief caught in his throat and made it impossible to say more. When he left that summer, a part of himself—the lighthearted, teasing friend—had stayed behind.

Mac had honored Jewel's wishes and stayed away for six long years. The really sad thing was, it had all been for nothing. She wasn't over what had happened. The past had not been forgotten.

He had often wondered if he'd done the wrong thing. Should he have told her parents the truth, anyway? Should he have come back the following summer? Should he have tried harder to get in touch with her over the years, to talk to her about what had happened?

A soft knock on the door forced Mac from his reverie. Before he could reply, the door opened, and Jewel stood silhouetted in the light from the hall. She was wearing a sleeveless white night-gown with a square-cut neck. The gown only covered her to mid-thigh. He could see the shape of her through the thin garment, the slender legs and slim waist and bountiful bosom.

He sat up, dragging the sheets around him to cover his nakedness and to conceal the sudden arousal caused by the enticing sight of her in his bedroom doorway. "Jewel? Is something wrong?"

She slipped inside and closed the door, so that momentarily he lost sight of her as his eyes adjusted to the dark. He heard the rustle of sheets and suddenly felt her body next to his beneath the covers.

"Jewel? What's going on?" He hoped his voice didn't sound as shocked as he felt. He didn't know what she thought she was doing, but he intended to find out before things went much farther.

He had expected an answer. He hadn't counted on her laying her palm on his bare chest. She followed that with a scattering of kisses across his chest that led her to the sensitive flesh beneath his ear. His body was trembling with desire when she finally paused to speak.

"Nothing's wrong, Mac," she murmured in

his ear. "I came because…" She nibbled on his earlobe, and he groaned at the exquisite pleasure of it. "I need your help," she finished.

He put an arm around her shoulder, realized suddenly he was naked and clutched at the sheet again. "Anything, Jewel. You know I'd do anything for you. But—"

"I was hoping you'd say that. Because what I need you to do… It won't be easy."

He waited, his breath caught in his chest, for what she had to say. "Anything, Jewel," he repeated, his heart thundering so loud he figured she could probably hear it.

She pressed her breasts against his chest and said, "I want you to make love to me."

His heart pounded, and his shaft pulsed. In another moment, things would be out of hand. His eyes had adapted to the dark, and with the moonlight from the window he at last could see the feelings etched on her face. Not desire, but fear and vulnerability.

"I want to feel like a woman," she said in a halting voice. "I want to stop being afraid."

He couldn't keep the dismay from his voice. "Aw, Jewel."

A cry of despair issued from her throat, and

she made a frantic lurch toward the edge of the bed and escape.

He grabbed for her, knowing she had misinterpreted his words. It wasn't that he didn't want her. He wanted her something fierce. He just wasn't the experienced bed partner she thought he was. He caught her by the wrist and pulled her back into his arms and held her tight, biting back a groan at the exquisite feel of her breasts crushed against his chest with only the sheer cloth between them.

"It's all right, Mac," she said in a brittle voice. "I made a mistake. Let me go, and we'll forget this ever happened."

She held herself stiff and unyielding in his arms. "Jewel—"

"Don't try to make me feel better. I deserve to feel like an idiot, throwing myself at you like this. I just thought…with all your experience…"

This time he did groan.

She tried to pull away, and he said, "You don't understand."

"I understand you don't find me attractive. I'm sorry for forcing myself on you like this."

"No!" *Tell her the truth, Macready. She's your friend. She'll understand.*

But the words stuck in his throat. If he hadn't

cared for her, if he didn't want her so badly, if things hadn't changed between them like they had, maybe he could have confessed the truth.

"It's not that I'm not attracted to you," he said.

He saw the look on her face and realized she didn't believe him. How could she not see the truth when it was throbbing like mad beneath the thin sheet that separated them?

"Then why won't you make love to me?" she challenged.

"Because…"

He couldn't tell her the truth, and he saw she believed the worst—that she had imposed herself where she wasn't wanted, and he was rejecting her as kindly as he could.

"Aw, Jewel," he said again. His voice was tender, as gentle as he wished he could be with her.

She made a keening sound in her throat, a mournful sound that made him ache somewhere deep inside.

He realized he had no choice. He had to try to make love to her. He couldn't botch things much worse than he already had. He leaned over and pressed his mouth against hers, restraining the rush of passion he felt at the touch of her soft, damp lips.

She moaned and arched her body against his. Her mouth clung to his, and he felt her need and her desire.

Maybe it's going to be all right. Maybe I can get us both through this.

He tried to hold back, so he wouldn't scare her. Yet when his tongue slipped into her mouth it found an eager welcome. He thrust deep, mimicking the sex act, and she riposted with her tongue in his mouth.

He thought the top of his head was going to come off. He had never felt so out of control. His hands slid down her arms, feeling the goose bumps and her shiver of anticipation. She was as excited as he was. She wanted him, too.

His lips started down her slender throat, across the silky flesh that led to her breastbone and downward, giving her plenty of warning where he was headed. She could have stopped him anytime she wanted. He wasn't an animal. He had his desire on a firm leash.

She cried out when his mouth latched onto her nipple, and he sucked hard through the cotton. Mac knew it wasn't a cry of fear, because her hands grasped his hair and held him there.

Her moan of pleasure urged him on. He released her breast momentarily and kissed her mouth again, an accolade for her trust in him. "I won't hurt you, Jewel. I would never hurt you," he murmured against her lips.

"I know, Mac. I know," she replied in gasping breaths.

Their tongues dueled dangerously, inciting them both to greater passion. He clasped her shoulders, making himself go slow, telling himself *Go Slow*. He slid his hand across the damp cotton that covered her breasts all the way down to her belly, wishing the damned nightgown wasn't between his palm and her flesh, but feeling the heat of her even through the thin shift.

He grabbed the bottom edge of it, anxious to get it out of his way, and brushed her thigh with his fingertips. Just her thigh. She tensed slightly but didn't pull away. He managed not to heave a sigh of relief.

It's going to be all right. I'll be able to do this for her.

But he was overeager and excited, worried about whether he would be able to satisfy her, and a moment later his hand accidentally brushed against the soft mound between her legs.

She jerked away from him with a cry of alarm. But he still had hold of the nightgown, and the fragile material tore. He let go, but it was too late. She was already rolled up in a tight, fetal ball with her back to him.

"Jewel—"

"I can't!" she cried. "I can't."

He laid a hand on her shoulder, and she cringed away.

"Please don't touch me," she whispered.

He lay staring at her in shock. He should have known better than to try this. He should have known he didn't have the experience to do it right. "What can I do?"

She turned to him, her eyes awash in despair. "I'm sorry, Mac."

"Aw, Jewel."

"I thought it would be all right. Because it was you," she sobbed. "Because you're my friend."

He would have to confess the truth. He owed her that much. "It isn't you, Jewel, it's me," he said flatly.

"You're just saying that to make me feel better," she said.

"No. I'm not." He forced himself to continue as she stared up at him. "You mustn't be discouraged by what happened here tonight. I'm sure another man, a more experienced man, could have managed things better. I lost control and frightened you.''

"But I trust you," she protested.

"All the more reason I should have kept my hands off of you." He huffed out a breath of air and shoved a hand through his hair in agitation.

"When you find a man you love," he said earnestly, "a man who loves you enough to take his time and do things right, I'm sure you'll be able to get past what happened to you."

She sat up slowly, her chin sunk to her chest, her hands knotted in front of her knees, which were clutched to her chest. She swallowed hard. "What you're saying is that you're not that man."

"No. I'm not."

"I see."

Evidently not. Evidently he hadn't hinted broadly enough at his inexperience for her to realize the truth.

Now it was too late. In the heat of the moment he might have confessed his virginity. But as his passion cooled, he felt appalled at how close he had come to exposing himself to her laughter.

And she would laugh. It would be gentle

laughter, kind laughter, an effervescent bubble of disbelief. But he couldn't bear to hear it.

"If you won't do this for me, I don't know where to turn," she said at last.

"There are lots of men out there who'd be attracted to you, if you'd let them see your charms."

She shot him a twisted smile. "You mean my Enormous Endowments?"

"I wouldn't call them that," he protested with a startled laugh.

"What would you call them?" She thrust her chest out, and his mouth went dry.

He hesitated a heartbeat and said, "Astonishing Assets?"

She laughed, the bubbly, effervescent sound he remembered from long ago. "Oh, God, now I've got you doing it!" She grabbed a pillow and hugged it tight against her ribs, effectively hiding the Generous Giants.

"Look, Jewel, for a start, you're going to have to stop doing that."

"Doing what?"

"Hiding behind clothes, behind your hair, behind pillows." He tugged on the pillow, and she reluctantly gave it up. He was immediately sorry, because it was hard to keep his eyes off her. He could see her brownish-pink nipples beneath the damp cloth.

"It was my breasts that got me into trouble in the first place," she said. "Can you blame me for wanting to hide them?"

"Maybe not," he conceded. "But hiding your light behind a bushel is not the way to find your Prince Charming. You're going to have to want to attract a man to find the right one."

"I'm afraid, Mac."

He saw that in her shadowed eyes. In her drawn features. From the instinctive way she circled her arms protectively around herself. But if he couldn't help her out by making love to her, the least he could do was help her find another man to do it.

"You can start small—no pun intended—and do this in baby steps. You've got to crawl before you can walk."

"Meaning?"

"Go back to basics, to flirting, to wanting to attract a man's attention."

"I can't do that."

"Can't? Or won't?"

"Won't."

"You can start with me," he coaxed. "I'll be your lab rat."

She grinned wryly. "Hold that thought. Man as rat. I like it."

He gave her a crooked smile. "The idea is for you to start seeing men as *men*—get it?"

"All right," she conceded with a sigh. "I'll give it a try. Where do I start?"

"Wear some clothes that fit better. Something that shows off—"

"My Plentiful Peaches?"

He laughed. "Actually, yeah, that would do it."

She slid her legs over the edge of the bad and looked back over her shoulder at him. "I'm not so sure about this, Mac."

"Believe me, it'll work," he said, wrapping the sheet around his waist as he rose to follow her to the door. "You'll have the guys around here on their knees begging to take you out."

She arched a skeptical brow. "You really think so?"

"I guarantee it."

She paused at the door and put a hand on his naked chest. His heart thudded. His loins throbbed. She searched his face, and he hoped his lurid thoughts weren't apparent.

"What if I attract the wrong kind of attention?'' she asked. "What if someone...some man..."

"Start here on the ranch. I'll keep an eye out for you. If any of the cowhands or counselors makes a wrong move, I'll be there. You can use me as your guinea pig."

"Hmm. Man as pig. I like that even better."

He laughed and tousled her hair. "Cut it out."

"You'll help me through this, won't you?" she asked, her heart in her eyes.

"If you want to try out your seductive wiles on someone safe, I'm your man," he volunteered. He would keep his libido in check if it killed him.

"You don't know how much that means to me, Mac. You really think this will work?"

"It's sure as hell worth a try."

"Thanks, Mac. Still friends?"

He wrapped his hand around her nape—to keep her at arm's distance—and said, "You bet. And don't worry. Anybody makes the wrong kind of move, I'll cut him off at the pass."

"My hero," she said, an impish grin forming on her lips.

"You bet." He knew he should shove her out the door and put temptation from his path, but he couldn't resist one last kiss.

He leaned down to her, keeping their bodies separated and pressed his mouth against hers with all the gentleness he could muster.

Her lips were pliant under his, soft and supple and incredibly sweet.

"Good night, Jewel. Go to bed and get some sleep."

"Good night, Mac. You, too."

He must have nodded, or grunted an assent, because she left the room and closed the door behind her. But he knew damned well he wasn't going to sleep.

Mac replayed the events of the evening in his head. If only he'd had more experience. If only his hand hadn't brushed against her and scared her. If only he'd known what to do to reassure her.

What was done was done. He'd had his chance and he'd blown it. The least he could do was help her find another guy to help her out, while keeping his own hormones in check. The last thing he wanted to do was scare her again. Which meant he'd better make sure she never found out her Beautiful Breasts turned him hard as a rock.

If she was going to start wearing clothes that fit, he'd better go shopping for some baggy jeans.

Chapter 7

Jewel decided the best way to avoid hiding behind her hair was to remove that option. She drove to the Stonecreek Ranch at the crack of dawn to have her sister Cherry whack it off. She had known Cherry would understand what she wanted to do and help her because, of all her adopted brothers and sisters, Cherry understood best what it meant to feel different.

Cherry was the last Whitelaw Brat to be adopted and had come to the family when she was fourteen, an extremely tall, redheaded, blue-eyed Irish girl—and an incorrigible juvenile delinquent. Jewel had been closest to her in age, only a year older. After a rocky start, during which Cherry did her best to break every rule— and offend every member—in the Whitelaw household, they had ended up becoming best friends.

The night Cherry was accused of spiking the punch bowl at the senior prom and expelled from high school, she had eloped with Billy Stonecreek to avoiding facing Zach and Rebecca. Cherry had become an instant mom to Billy's twin six-year-old daughters Raejean and Annie. Three years later, Cherry was six months pregnant, and as far as Jewel could tell, happy as a cat in a dairy.

Cherry had made the Stonecreek Ranch a comfortable place to live, substituting leather and wood furniture for the silks and satins bought by Billy's first wife, Laura, who had died in a car accident. Jewel was surprised, when she showed up at Cherry's back screen door unannounced, to catch her sister and brother-in-law kissing in the kitchen.

It wasn't the kiss that shocked her. It was the passion behind it. Billy's hands avidly cupped Cherry's breasts, and her hands clutched his buttocks. They were pressed together like flies on flypaper.

She cleared her throat noisily. "Excuse me."

Jewel imagined a ripping sound as they sprang apart.

"Jewel!" Cherry exclaimed, her voice revealing both relief and irritation. "What are you doing here?"

"Obviously interrupting something important," Jewel said with a teasing grin.

Her sister flushed a delightful pink, and Billy stuck his hands in his front pockets, a move that didn't do as much as he probably hoped to hide his state of arousal.

Jewel felt a little guilty for intruding, and if it hadn't been an emergency she might have turned and left. But she was afraid she would lose her nerve if she waited. She stepped into the kitchen, careful not to let the screen door slam behind her and wake the twins. "I need my hair cut. Could you do it for me?"

"Now?" Cherry asked, her brows rising practically to her hairline.

"Yes, now."

Jewel was wearing a sleeveless white knit shell and tight-fitting jeans that had been shut away in a drawer for six years. She watched as

Cherry perused her attire and exchanged a look with Billy, whose eyes had opened wide with astonishment once she stepped inside. Jewel resisted the urge to cross her arms over her chest. She was going to have to get used to men looking at her.

"Hi, Billy," she said.

"Hi, Jewel." It came out as a croak. He cleared his throat and tried again. "You look..." He searched for a word and came up with, "Nice. What's the occasion?"

He was clearly curious, as she suspected her family would be, about why she was suddenly exposing assets she had kept hidden for the past six years. "No occasion," she said. "I just want to get my hair cut. Can you help me out?" she asked Cherry.

"Sure," Cherry said. She turned to Billy. "You don't mind if we postpone breakfast for half an hour, do you?"

"I've got some chores I can do in the barn. Give a holler when you want me." Billy grabbed his Stetson from the antler rack on the wall and headed out the screen door. Cherry caught it before it could slam.

"All right," Cherry said once she had scissors in hand and Jewel was settled in a kitchen chair with a towel around her shoulders. "Spill the jelly beans. What's going on?"

"Nothing much."

"For the first time in six years I can see you have breasts," Cherry retorted tartly. "Believe me, anyone seeing your breasts for the first time wouldn't say they're 'nothing much.'"

Jewel laughed. That was why she liked Cherry so much. She didn't pull her punches. Cherry said exactly what she was thinking, even if it wasn't necessarily what you wanted to hear.

"I had a talk with Mac Macready last night," Jewel said. "He convinced me it's time to come out of my shell."

"I see," Cherry said.

Jewel realized Cherry was *seeing* a great deal more than she wished or intended. "It isn't like that."

"Like what?"

"It's not Mac I'm trying to attract."

"It isn't?"

"No. Not that I don't love him dearly. I do. As a friend."

"A *friend*," Cherry repeated.

Jewel winced as nine-inch-long hanks of brown hair began falling to the kitchen floor.

There was no turning back now. "A friend," she confirmed.

"And this *friend* suggested you'd look better in skin-tight jeans and short hair?"

Jewel laughed. "Not exactly. He simply said I should dress to attract a man."

"What you're wearing ought to do it," Cherry confirmed.

"You think so? It's not too...enticing?"

"You're dressed fine, Jewel. Half the young women in this country are probably wearing similar outfits this morning. You can't help it if you have big breasts."

Jewel noticed Cherry said it without the capital B's. Jewel automatically thought Big Breasts, something she was going to have to get over if she was going to have any hope of surviving this metamorphosis.

"There," Cherry said, surveying her handiwork. "A few turns with my curling iron, and I think you'll be pleased with the result."

When Cherry was done, she held a mirror in front of Jewel's face. "Take a look."

Her hair swept along her chin in a shiny bob, with soft bangs across her brow. Jewel sighed. "Oh, Cherry, you're a marvel. I look—"

"Cute," Cherry said with an irreverent laugh. "No getting around it. You're darned cute."

"I'm twenty-two. That's too old for cute. Besides, my features are too ordinary to be—"

"Cute," Cherry persisted with a grin. "Let me call Billy, and he can confirm it." She called out the door for Billy, who bounded up the back steps and into the kitchen.

He paused in the acting of pulling off his leather work gloves as he looked Jewel up and down. "Who would've believed a haircut could make such a difference?"

"Isn't she cute?" Cherry asked.

"Sexy," Billy countered. When his wife nudged him in the ribs, he amended, "Sexy and cute."

Jewel's brow furrowed. She had never been pretty, and "cute" sounded like something you said about a one-year-old with a lollipop. One glance down explained the "sexy." Jewel felt the heat start in her throat and work its way up her neck to sit like red flags on her cheeks. "Good God," she said. "Have you got an extra shirt I can borrow?" she asked Billy.

"What for?" Billy said.

"She wants to go back into hiding," Cherry said scornfully. "Well, we're not going to help you do it. You turn right around and head out that door with your head held high. You've got nothing to be ashamed of. What happened to you six years ago wasn't your fault. It's about time you shoved Harvey Barnes out of your life and started enjoying it again.''

"That's pretty much what Mac said."

"Good for Mac," Cherry said. "Am I going to have to go with you to make sure you don't cover yourself up like a nun?"

"No," Jewel conceded with a chagrined look. "I'll be all right."

"Stand up straight and enjoy the looks you get. Because you darn sure deserve them!''

"Thanks, Cherry," Jewel said, giving her sister a quick hug. "Thanks for everything."

Her brother-in-law gave her a quick hug and teased, "Definitely sexy. Go get 'em, Jewel."

Cherry and Billy stood arm in arm on the back porch waving as she drove away. They were already kissing again as the dust rose behind her pickup.

It wasn't easy resisting the urge to slip a long-sleeved shirt over the figure-exposing knit shell the instant she returned home. It would have been easier if Mac had been there waiting, and she could have gotten that first meeting over with.

But he wasn't there.

She had left a note hanging on Mac's door when she snuck out to get her hair cut. The note she found stuck on her door when she got back said that he had taped up his ankle and gone walking despite the sprain. She left a third note for Mac saying that she was eating breakfast with her family and inviting him to join them, then left the cottage before she lost her courage.

Jewel figured it couldn't hurt to have a buffer between her and Mac when he saw her for the first time in her new guise. Not that she thought he wouldn't approve. After all, it had been his idea for her to feature her assets more prominently. But after last night...

In the bright light of day, Jewel found it hard to believe she had crossed the hall to Mac's bedroom last night. Or that she had actually asked him to make love to her. Or that he had refused.

She wished he had done it before kissing her. Good Lord. Who would have thought a kiss from Mac Macready could turn her to mush like that? His lips had been soft and slightly damp, and he had tasted...like Mac. Familiar and good.

If that was all she had felt, she would never

have gotten frightened the way she had. But there had also been something dark and dangerous about his kisses. A threat of leashed passion that once freed might... When Mac had accidentally touched her, that awful sense of powerlessness had returned, and the bad memories had all come crashing down on her.

She couldn't blame Mac for backing away like he had. What man wouldn't cut his losses? Mac had gently but firmly told her to find somebody else to make love to her. He wasn't available for the job.

She didn't want somebody else, she had realized. She wanted Mac. Which was why she was dressed like this. Cherry had seen right through her feeble protests. The only man she wanted to attract was Mac Macready. She would never have found the courage to shed her protective skin of clothing if she hadn't conceded this was one sure way of getting Mac's attention.

He had certainly seemed interested last night. That is, before she had gotten scared and scared him off. Before he had accidentally touched her below the waist, everything had been wonderful. Her knee-jerk reaction had come before her rational mind could tell her it was Mac.

That had been followed by the disturbing

thought that maybe even Mac couldn't make it all right. That maybe she would forever fear a man's touch in bed. She had kept herself curled up in a ball to avoid testing the truth. Because that possibility was too devastating to contemplate.

Jewel was determined to get over her fear. She was determined to give Mac another chance. And she wanted Mac to want another chance. She was understandably nervous about her next meeting with him. It made a lot of sense to diffuse the situation by including her family in the equation. Hence the unusual visit to her family's breakfast table. This morning she needed the support they had always given her. She wanted their reassurance that she looked all right, that she would not "stick out" in a crowd.

Jewel could smell biscuits and bacon through the screen door. She smiled and stepped inside, knowing she would find the warmth of hearth and home. She stopped just inside the door, enjoying the cacophony of seven voices—Rolleen was away at medical school—raised in excited chatter.

"Wow! You look different!"

Jewel smiled self-consciously at Colt as she settled into an empty chair at the breakfast table.

She was tempted to slump down, but forced herself to sit up straight. This was the new and improved Jewel Whitelaw.

Her mom gave her a bright smile and said, "You look lovely today, sweetheart."

"Why'd you cut off all your—"

Nineteen-year-old Jake elbowed fifteen-year-old Rabbit to shut him up. "You look real nice, Jewel," Jake said. He exchanged a knowing look with their father at the head of the table.

Jewel felt her cheeks heating. They had noticed the difference, all right, but so far had avoided commenting directly on it. She decided to keep their attention focused on her hair. "It's been so hot lately, I decided to get a trim," she said to appease the curious looks she was getting from sixteen-year-old Frannie and twenty-year-old Avery.

"Good idea," her father said, buttering a fluffy biscuit.

"I've got some time this morning if you need any last-minute help getting ready for the first drove of campers," her mother offered, as she set a bowl of scrambled eggs and a second platter of bacon in the center of the table.

"Everything's under control, Mom," Jewel said.

"When do you go to the airport?" her father asked.

"The flight from Dallas arrives at 9:30 this morning with about a half-dozen kids," she replied. "There's another half dozen and the two counselors arriving from Houston shortly afterward. Mac has volunteered to go with me in the van to pick them up. I invited him to join us for breakfast," she said. "I hope that's all right."

"Of course it's all right," her mother replied. "It'll be nice to visit with him. We've barely seen hide or hair of either of you. What have you been doing?"

"Mac's been walking in the mornings—"

"Is his ankle better?" Colt asked.

"What's wrong with his ankle?" her father asked.

Colt got busy scooping another spoonful of eggs on his plate and sent a pleading look toward Jewel not to betray him.

"He tripped and twisted it yesterday," Jewel said. "It seems to be all right this morning."

"It's fine," Mac said as he opened the screen door and stepped into the kitchen. "How's everyone this morning?"

He was greeted with a chorus of smiles and "hellos" and "hi's."

Jewel feasted her eyes on him. His blond hair was still damp from the shower, and the rugged planes of his face were shadowed by a day's growth of beard, so he hadn't even stopped to shave. He must have been afraid of missing breakfast. He was wearing a Western shirt tucked into beltless, butter-soft jeans and cowboy boots.

She looked up at him defiantly, daring him not to like what he saw. He was the one who had wanted change. She had provided it. He had better not complain.

Jewel saw nothing in his blue eyes but admiration. That flustered her as much, and perhaps more than the opposite reaction. She hadn't been ready for the blatant male appreciation of her figure that she found on his face.

"I hope I'm not too late for breakfast," he said as he slipped into the last empty chair, which happened to be across from Jewel.

"Just in time," Zach said.

Jewel could feel Mac's eyes on her but kept her gaze lowered as she ate her scrambled eggs. It was going to take some time for her to adjust to having men look at her with sexual interest. It was all right when Mac did it, because she did not feel frightened by him. But he was right. If she wanted to get over the past, this was a start in the right direction.

She heard Mac exchange comments with her father about the cattle and cutting horse businesses that supported Hawk's Pride, listened to him discuss football with Colt, smiled along with him as he teased Rabbit about his nickname, which dated from his childhood when he had loved carrots. Mac obviously knew her family well, and they apparently liked him as much as he liked them.

Jewel felt a rush of guilt at having deprived Mac of their company all these years. Having been Mac's friend, she knew how hard it was for his own family to treat him normally. His parents and older sister, Sadie, had hovered over him long after he was well, afraid to let him try things for fear he would get hurt and end up back in the hospital.

Zach and Rebecca loved Mac like a son, but they hadn't spent years with him in a hospital setting where he was fighting for his life against a disease that killed kids. They were willing to let him do a man's work. Jewel knew Mac had needed his summers as a counselor at Camp LittleHawk as much as Zach and Rebecca had needed his help with the kids.

"Right, Jewel?"

Jewel looked up at Mac, startled to realize he was speaking to her. "Excuse me. I wasn't listening. What was the question?"

Her family laughed.

"What's so funny?" she demanded, looking at them suspiciously.

"I said the reason the kids keep coming back year after year is that you're constantly making changes to keep things interesting," Mac said with a grin.

Jewel realized that this year she had made a huge change that was bound to be noticed—by the other counselors, if not the kids. One of the reasons she loved working with kids was that they never seemed to notice her ample bosom. "Change is good," she said, both chin and chest outthrust defiantly.

"Of course it is, darling," her mother said in a soothing voice.

"I wasn't complaining, Jewel," Mac said, his gaze staying level with hers.

She kept waiting for it to drop to her breasts. But it never did. There was nothing sexual in his gaze now. What she saw was approval and appreciation of her as a person. A thickness in her throat made it hard to speak. "We'd better get going," she said. "We don't want to be late to the airport."

"I'm ready when you are," Mac said, pushing back from the table. "Thanks for the breakfast, Rebecca. I don't know when I've enjoyed a meal so much. It's great to be back."

"It's great to have you back," Zach said, rising and putting a hand on Mac's shoulder as he walked him to the door." You're welcome anytime."

"Thanks, Zach," Mac said, shaking hands with the older man.

Jewel felt exposed once she and Mac emerged from the throng of hugging and backslapping brothers and sisters and parents and headed across the backyard toward the van.

She felt Mac's gaze trained on her again, intense, disturbing, because this time he was obviously looking at more than her face. She paused as soon as they were hidden by a large bougainvillea and turned to confront him.

She propped her balled hands on her hips, thrust her shoulders back and held her chin high. "All right, Mac. You were the one who asked for this. Look your fill and get it over with."

His lips curved. His eyes surveyed her intently. His voice turned whiskey rough as he said, "You could stand there till doomsday, and I wouldn't get my fill of looking at you."

Jewel would have scoffed, but the sound got caught in her throat. "Mac..."

He stepped close enough to put them toe to toe.

She struggled not to give ground. "Say what you think. Spit it out. I can take it."

His thumb caressed the faint scars on her bared cheek, then edged into her hair. "Your hair's so soft. So shiny. So sleek." His hand slid through her hair to capture her nape and hold her still as he lowered his head. "I find you irresistible, Jewel."

Jewel felt her heart thudding, had trouble catching her breath, then stopped breathing altogether as his mouth closed over hers.

He kept their bodies separated, touching her only with his mouth. The searing kiss was enough to curl her toes inside her boots.

He lifted his head and said, "Welcome back, Jewel. I missed the old you."

"Oh, Mac—" She was on the verge of blurting out her strong feelings for him—the same feelings his kiss had suggested he had for her—when he interrupted.

"I don't think you're going to have any trou-

ble at all attracting the man of your dreams.''
He smile ruefully. ''You're going to have to remind me to keep my distance. I don't want any
good prospects to think I have any kind of claim
on you except as a friend.''

Jewel stared at him with stunned eyes, but
quickly recovered her composure. ''No sweat,
Mac,'' she said, turning and heading for the van.
''I'll make sure any men I meet know exactly
where you stand.''

She owed Mac too much to make him feel
uncomfortable by revealing her new feelings for
him before he was ready to hear them. But if
kissing her like this only reinforced the bonds of
friendship, she had her work cut out for her. The
changes in her hair and wardrobe had been use-
ful in helping Mac to see her as a desirable female. All she had to do now was figure out how
to make him fall in love with her.

Chapter 8

Mac stared out the window of the van at the flat grassland that lined the road between Hawk's Pride and the airport, rather than at the woman behind the wheel. But he very much wanted to feast his eyes on Jewel.

He liked the bouncy new haircut that showed off the line of her chin and made her cheekbones more prominent. He liked the formfitting clothes that outlined a lush figure he yearned to hold close to his own. He was intrigued by the sparkle of wonder and delight—and unfulfilled promise—in her dark brown eyes.

Mac wished he had a Stetson to set on his lap.

He hadn't realized he would be so physically susceptible to the striking change in Jewel's appearance. A friend would have settled for giving her an approving pat on the back. His kiss had been a purely male impulse, an effort to stake his claim on an intensely desirable female.

Mac recognized his problem. He simply had no idea how to solve it. How did a man stop desiring a woman? Especially one he not only lusted after but also liked very much?

Jewel sat across from him behind the wheel not saying a word. But speaking volumes.

Tension radiated between them. Sexual tension.

He had told her to find another man, but now he wasn't so sure. She had certainly seemed to enjoy his kiss. Maybe if he seduced her in stages... If they took it slow and easy...

Who was he kidding? When it came down to the nitty-gritty, it was still going to be the first time for him. He was still going to be guessing at what he was doing. Besides, it wasn't fair to change his mind at this late date.

Who said life was fair?

"I appreciate you coming along to help today," Jewel said, interrupting his thoughts.

"My pleasure. How many people are we picking up?"

"Twelve kids, two counselors."

"Are you still hiring college kids?"

"Patty Freeburg is still in college. Gavin Talbot is in graduate school. I should warn you, this group of kids includes Brad Templeton."

"The kid who wanted to meet me?"

Jewel nodded. "His leukemia is in its second remission. You know how that works. You're afraid to get your hopes up that this remission will last, because you've already slipped out of remission once."

"You have to keep believing you can beat the disease," Mac said.

"Most kids aren't as lucky as you were."

"You think it was luck that I beat myelocytic leukemia?" he asked.

"Statistics say the chances of a kid surviving that kind of leukemia aren't good. What else could it have been?"

"Sheer determination. Willpower. It can move mountains. Recently it put me back on my own two feet when the doctors said I would never walk again without a brace."

"Granted, willpower is important. Determination counts for a lot. But are they enough to get your leg back into shape for pro football?'' Jewel asked.

Mac felt a spurt of panic. "Sure. Why not?"

"Willpower can't replace the missing muscle in your leg, Mac. Determination can't make the scars disappear."

"I can compensate."

She nodded. "For your sake, I hope so."

"Why are you being so negative about this?" Mac demanded, using anger to force back the fear that had surfaced with her doubts.

"I'm not being negative, just realistic. You learn to accept—"

"Don't accept anything that isn't exactly what you want. Don't expect anything less than the best for yourself or those sick kids, Jewel. You deserve it. And so do they."

Jewel smiled ruefully. "To tell the truth, this is an argument I don't want to win. I want to believe in happily ever after for these kids and for you. And I'm hoping desperately for it myself. I've taken the first steps toward a new me. I have to admit it feels good, even though it is a little scary."

He met her glance briefly and saw the fear, before she returned her gaze to the road in front of her. "Why scary?"

"Because I'm not sure how well I'll handle all the male attention once I have it."

"Encourage the men you're interested in, and discourage the ones you don't want."

She grunted her disgust. "You make it sound so easy. Encourage how? Discourage how?"

"Smiles. And frowns."

Jewel looked at him incredulously, then gave a bubbly laugh. "If it were only that simple!"

"It is," Mac assured her.

She eyed him doubtfully. "That's all there is to it?"

"Why not try an experiment? When this Gavin What's-his-name—"

"Talbot," Jewel provided.

"When Talbot gets off the plane, give him a 'You're the one!' smile, and see what kind of response you get."

They had arrived at the local airport just as the commuter plane from Dallas was landing. Jewel stopped the van close to the terminal and stepped out to wait for the plane door to open and the kids to come down the portable stairs to the tarmac.

The three girls and four boys on the Dallas flight all wore hats of some kind, a means of hiding the ravages of chemotherapy on their hair. Baseball caps, berets, slouch hats, straw hats, bandannas, Jewel had seen them all. Beneath the hats their eyes looked haunted, their mouths grim. Jewel looked forward to easing their worries for two weeks, to helping them forget for a short time that their lives were threatened with extinction.

A scuffle broke out between two of the boys the instant they reached the tarmac. The other kids spread out in a circle to watch.

"Hey!" Jewel cried, running to reach them.

Mac was there before her and picked up the boy who had done the shoving, leaving the other boy with no one to fight. "What's the problem?" Mac asked in a calm voice.

The boy on the tarmac was in tears. He pointed to the boy in Mac's arms. "He said I'm going to die."

"We're all going to die," Mac replied. "Could get hit by a bus tomorrow."

The other kids smiled. It was an old joke for them, but it still worked every time.

The crying boy was not amused. He pointed to the kid in Mac's arms. "He said I can't beat it. He said no one can. He said—"

Mac perused the thin, gangly boy held snug against his side. "Doesn't look like a doctor to me," he said. "Where do you suppose he got the information to make his diagnosis? You a doctor?" Mac asked the kid.

The boy clenched his teeth and said nothing.

"Guess that settles that," Mac said. "Any other questions?" he asked the crying boy.

The kid wiped his nose on the shoulder of his T-shirt and pulled his Harwell Grain and Feed cap snugly over his eyes. "Guess not."

Mac exchanged a look with Jewel, who began herding the children toward the terminal.

"Why don't you all come inside with me," she said. "We'll get a soda while we wait for the kids from Houston to arrive, along with your counselors."

As soon as they were gone, Mac set the boy down on his feet in front of him. Knowing the kid would likely run the instant he let go, Mac settled onto one knee, his hands trapping the kid's frail shoulders, and tried to see the boy's eyes under his baseball cap. The kid's chin was tucked so close to his chest, it was impossible.

"What's your name?" Mac asked.

"I want to go home."

"You sound pretty mad."

"I never wanted to come here in the first place. My mom made me!"

"Why'd you tell that boy he was going to die?"

"'Cause he is!"

"Who says?"

"He's got acute myelocytic leukemia, same as me. It kills you for sure!"

"I'm not dead."

The boy's chin jerked up, and his pale blue eyes focused on Mac's. "You're not sick."

"I was. Same as you."

The boy shook his head. "But you're—"

"I'm Mac Macready."

The blue eyes widened. "*You're* him? You look different from the picture on your trading card."

"I was younger then," Mac replied. *And twenty pounds heavier with muscle.*

"My mom said you'd be here, but I didn't believe her."

"You must be Brad Templeton." Mac let go of the kid's shoulders, rose and stuck out his hand. "Nice to meet you, Brad."

The boy stared at Mac's hand suspiciously before he laid his own tiny palm against it. Mac figured the kid for eleven or twelve, but he didn't look much more than eight or nine. The slight body, the gaunt cheeks, the hopeless look in his eyes, told how the disease had decimated him—body and soul.

"You ready to join the others?" Mac asked.

He watched as the boy looked toward the kids bunched in the front window of the terminal and made a face. "This is a waste of time."

"Why is that?"

"I mean, why bother pretending everything is all right, when it's not?"

Mac put a hand on the boy's back, and they began walking toward the terminal. "Why not pretend? Why not enjoy every moment you've got?"

The boy met his gaze, and Mac knew the answer without having to hear it. He had been through it all himself.

This was a child going through the stages that prepared him for death. The anger. The grieving. And finally, the acceptance. Brad Templeton had done it all before, when the first remission ended. Then death had given him a brief reprieve—a second remission. But having once accepted the fact he was going to die, it was awfully hard to start living all over again.

"Death doesn't always win," Mac said quietly.

Brad looked up at him. "How did you beat it?"

"Determination. Willpower."

Brad shook his head. "That isn't enough. If it was, I'd already be well."

"Don't give up."

"I have to," Brad said. "It hurts too bad to hope when you know it isn't going to make any difference."

They had reached the door to the terminal, but before going inside, Mac stooped down and turned the boy to face him. "Sometimes you have to forget about what the doctors say and believe in yourself."

Brad looked skeptical.

Mac didn't know who he was trying to convince, himself or the kid. Sometimes the doctors were right. Kids died. And football players got career-ending injuries.

He rose and said, "Come on, Brad. We can keep each other company this week and have some fun."

Brad snorted. "Fun. Yeah. Right."

Mac smiled. "If you're not smiling ear to ear when you get back on that plane in two weeks, I'll—"

"How are you two doing?" Jewel interrupted.

A whoosh of cold air escaped the terminal as she joined them in the Texas heat that was already rising from the tarmac.

"I was making a bet with Brad that he would be smiling by the end of next week."

Brad grimaced.

Jewel eyed Brad, then murmured to Mac, "Looks like you have your work cut out for you."

"Come on, Brad," Mac said, giving the boy a nudge toward the door. "Let's go inside and meet the other kids."

"I've already met them," Brad said sullenly. "They all hate me."

"We'll have to work on that, too," Mac said, sending Jewel a look that said "Help!" over his shoulder.

"I'd appreciate it if you'd keep an eye on everybody while I greet the folks on the plane from Houston," she said.

Mac realized the second commuter plane had arrived, Jewel was headed back out onto the tarmac. "Don't forget," he said. "Smile."

Jewel shot him a radiant smile. "How's this?"

Mac put an exaggerated hand to his heart. "Lord have mercy, girl, that's potent stuff!"

Jewel laughed and turned away, her hips swaying seductively in the tight jeans.

Mac was glad she'd turned away when she had. His hand was still on his heart, but it was keeping the damned thing from flying out of his chest. If she kept walking like that, he wasn't going to be able to go inside anytime soon.

He felt a tug on his shirtsleeve and looked down to see Brad staring up at him.

"You got the hots for her?"

Mac stared, agog. "The *hots?*"

"You know. Sexy chick like that—"

Mac put a hand over Brad's mouth. "Where did a kid your age learn—? Don't answer that. She's Miss Whitelaw to you."

The kid reached up to uncover his mouth. "I'm twelve. I was here when I was nine and Jewel said we can call her Jewel and she's a lot prettier now."

"And you're old enough to notice, is that it?"

Brad gave Mac a man-to-man shrug. "I haven't thought too much about girls 'cause... you know."

Mac put a hand on Brad's shoulder. "Yeah, I know how that is, too."

He ushered Brad inside thinking it was going to be a very long two weeks.

* * *

Jewel's heart was beating rapidly. Even kidding the way he was, Mac's admiring look had been enough to take her breath away. It was easy to keep the smile on her face long enough to greet the other five campers, Patty Freeburg and Gavin Talbot.

Patty was petite and pretty, with long blond hair she wore in a youthful ponytail, blue eyes and a wonderfully open smile. "Hello," she said. "I'm glad to be back."

"Good to have you back, Patty," Jewel said. "You know the drill. Would you mind helping the kids locate their luggage inside?"

"Sure," Patty said. "Come on, you guys, hup, two, three, four!"

The two boys marched, and the three girls giggled as they followed Patty toward the terminal.

Jewel turned to greet Gavin Talbot, who was hefting a duffel bag over his shoulder. She knew Gavin's credentials backward and forward. He was twenty-six and working on a Ph.D. in child psychology. Eventually he planned to become a clinical psychologist, and work with dying kids. He was spending time at Camp LittleHawk because it catered to children with cancer.

She knew Gavin would have to be an empathetic and caring man to choose such a career. She had not imagined he would also be stunningly handsome.

He was over six feet tall, with the sort of rangy body Jewel was used to seeing on cowhands, who led physically active lives. His sun-streaked, tobacco-brown hair suggested a lot of time out-of-doors, and the spray of tan lines around his dark brown eyes confirmed it. He was dressed in a white, oxford-cloth shirt, unbuttoned at the throat and turned up to his forearms, well-worn—though not ragged—jeans and cowboy boots.

"Hello, Miss Whitelaw," he said, reaching out to shake her hand as they followed Patty and the kids back to the terminal.

His large, callused hand engulfed hers, offering comfort, reassurance and something else...a spark of sexual interest.

Jewel didn't think she was imagining it. She felt a small frisson of pleasure merely from his firm handclasp. It was probably the way he looked into her eyes, as though seeking a connection, that made her insides jump a little.

"Call me Jewel, please, Gavin," she replied.

"Jewel," he repeated, the smile broadening, becoming more relaxed. "The name fits."

Jewel only had an instant to decide whether to frown or smile, as Mac had instructed. Jewel smiled.

She had only taken two steps when Gavin put a hand under her elbow and said, "You're hurt."

"It's an old injury that causes me to limp," she said, wondering if the interest she had previously seen would diminish, now that he knew she was considerably less than perfect.

Her opinion of him went up a notch when he said, "It doesn't seem to slow you down much."

She felt a spurt of anxiety when Gavin made eye contact with her again, because the sexual spark was still there. Well, she had wanted to attract him and she had. So now what did she do with him? She turned to find Mac staring at her through the terminal's front picture window.

Mac was safe. Mac was nonthreatening.

Mac also was not volunteering to help her get over the lingering fear that had kept her celibate all these years. Maybe seeing that someone else was interested in her would spur him to action.

She turned back to Gavin and forced another

smile onto her face. "You look like you spend a lot of time outdoors."

"I own a cattle ranch south of Houston," he said. "I spend my weekends there when I can."

"You should be right at home here," she said. "We do a lot of trail rides in the early morning and late afternoon for the children."

"What about moonlight rides for the grown-ups?" he asked. "Ending with a romantic camp-fire and toasted marshmallows?"

Jewel was a little shocked at how fast Gavin had made his move. She swallowed back the knot of fear and shot him a calculated come-hither glance. "I suppose that could be ar-ranged."

"How about tonight?"

"How about what tonight?" Mac asked.

Jewel had been so busy staring back into Gavin's brown eyes, she hadn't realized they had reached the terminal. Mac's question caught her unawares. "What?"

"Jewel and I were just setting up a moonlight ride for tonight," Gavin said.

Jewel heard the warning in Gavin's voice. *Stay clear. This one's mine. We don't want com-pany.*

Mac ignored it. "Sounds like a fine idea," he

said. "Hey, Patty, you want to go for a moon-light ride tonight?"

Patty smiled. "Sure. Who all's going?"

"Everybody," Gavin said wryly, his gaze never leaving Mac's.

At least Gavin was a good sport, Jewel thought. She was grateful that Mac had realized how uncomfortable she would have been all alone with Gavin and had invited himself and Patty. With Mac along she would feel safer flirting with Gavin. And perhaps Mac would be moved to do a little flirting himself.

Jewel was amused to see how Gavin maneuvered to be in the front seat with her on the trip back, forcing Mac into the back with Patty and the kids. Gavin wasn't the least impressed by Mac's football hero status, because he wasn't a big football fan.

"I know that sounds like blasphemy in Texas," he said. "But I'd rather spend my Saturday and Sunday afternoons at the ranch, since I'm stuck indoors reading and writing the rest of the week."

"What's the name of your ranch?" Jewel asked as she started the van and headed back toward the ranch.

"Let's not talk about me," Gavin said, avoiding an answer. "Tell me about yourself."

Jewel watched Gavin stiffen as Mac suddenly leaned forward, bracing his arms on the back of the front seat, effectively interposing himself between Jewel and the counselor. "Mind if I listen?" Mac said. "Jewel and I haven't had much time to catch up on things since the last time we were together."

Jewel heard the insinuation in Mac's voice that suggested "together" meant more than sitting on a garden swing next to each other.

"You two are old friends?" Gavin asked, eyeing the two of them speculatively.

"We're rooming together," Mac said. "Didn't Jewel tell you?"

Jewel turned a fiery red at the knowing look Gavin gave her, even though the situation with Mac was perfectly innocent. She was a little perturbed at Mac. He seemed to be saying everything he could to keep Gavin at a distance. She appreciated his concern, but until he volunteered to take Gavin's place, she was determined to be brave enough to pursue the relationship.

She forced a laugh and said, "Mac has been like a big brother to me for years. He gets a little protective at times."

Gavin's brows rose, and the smile returned. "I see. Don't worry, Mac," he said, patting Mac's arm. "I'll take good care of her."

Mac grunted and shifted back into the back seat, his arms crossed over his chest.

Jewel shivered as she made brief eye contact with Gavin. It looked like she was going to get a chance to try out her feminine wiles tonight. Mac would be there, so she wouldn't have to worry about things getting out of hand. Toasting marshmallows over a campfire would be a marvelously romantic setting, perfect for establishing a friendly rapport with Gavin.

She wondered if Gavin would try to kiss her. She wondered if she should let him. She caught Mac's narrowed gaze in the rearview mirror and wondered, with a smile, if *Mac* would let him. She had better have a talk with Mac before the trail ride and let him know she welcomed Gavin's attentions for the practice they would provide.

Jewel shivered in anticipation. She only hoped that when the time came, and Gavin made advances, she would have the nerve to follow through.

Chapter 9

Mac stared through his horse's ears at Jewel, riding side by side with Gavin on the moonlit trail ahead of him. Patty had decided to stay at the ranch, so he had no riding partner. Mac watched Jewel lean close to hear what Gavin was saying. A trilling burble of laughter floated back to him on the wind. His neck hairs rose, and he gritted his teeth in frustration.

That could have been him riding beside Jewel. That could have been him making her laugh. Instead, he was reduced to the role of chaperon. And not enjoying it one bit.

Mac turned to see who was coming as another horse cantered up beside him bearing one of the three late additions to their trail ride. "Hey, Colt. What's new?"

"You know anything about that Gavin guy?" Colt asked, aiming his chin toward the couple ahead of them.

Mac stared at Gavin. "He's as comfortable on a horse as any cowboy I've ever seen, he's educated, friendly, courteous and he appears to be interested in Jewel."

"You think he'll try to hurt her?"

Mac saw the worry on Colt's young face. Six years ago the kid had been only eight, but obviously Jewel's trauma had left a lasting impression on her family. "There's not much Gavin can do with me along," Mac reassured the teenager.

Colt heaved a sigh of relief. "Thanks, Mac. Jewel is...well, she's pretty special."

"I know."

Colt glanced over his shoulder, frowned, then looked straight ahead again. "I thought I might get to see a little more of Jenny if we came along tonight. I should have known she'd stick like glue to Huck."

Mac arched a brow. "You have feelings for her yourself?"

Colt readjusted his Western straw hat, setting it lower over his eyes to hide his expression. "She's Huck's girl."

"You didn't answer my question."

"So what if I like her?" Colt retorted. "Nothing's gonna come of it. They'll probably get married as soon as Huck finishes college."

"College is a long way off. Maybe Huck will change his mind. Or Jenny will."

Colt snorted. "What difference would that make? She doesn't know I'm alive."

Mac wasn't sure what to say. He hadn't been too fortunate in the romance department himself. But he knew what he would do if he loved a woman. "Mind if I offer you some advice?"

Colt shrugged.

"If you get a chance to make Jenny your girl, grab it with both hands." He grinned at Colt. "It's awful hard for a woman to resist a man who loves her, heart and soul."

Colt eyed him sideways. "If you say so."

They had reached the ring of stones Camp LittleHawk used as a campfire site for barbecues. Mac watched as Gavin lifted Jewel from her horse, sliding her down the front of him as he settled her feet on the ground. He saw the stunned look on Jewel's face as she gazed up at Gavin. Was it fear or wonder she had felt at the intimate contact?

He kneed his horse into a lope to catch up to them. He was out of the saddle and at her side seconds later. "Hey, Jewel," he said, putting a hand on her shoulder. "Let's get the fire going for those marshmallows."

When she looked at him, he saw dazed pleasure in her eyes. Damn. She was definitely aroused. A quick glance at the front of her—at the pebbled nipples that showed through the knit top—confirmed his diagnosis.

So what was he supposed to do now? Disappear, so Gavin could get on with his seduction?

The hell he would.

He grabbed Jewel's hand. "Come on, Jewel. Let's get some firewood."

Jewel glanced at him in surprise, smiled and followed him to the box of firewood that was kept nearby. He loaded her arms with kindling and picked up a few logs to carry back himself. By the time they returned to the fire, Colt had unpacked the wire clothes hangers they had brought along and was unbending them to make marshmallow roasting sticks.

Mac and Jewel knelt together before the ring of stones that Jenny and Huck were straightening and began arranging the kindling and logs. Gavin arrived moments later with the bag of marshmallows, a thermos of hot chocolate and some paper cups from his saddlebag and a couple of blankets that had been tied behind Jewel's saddle.

"Up, you two," he said to Mac and Jewel. "Let me get this down under you."

Mac and Jewel scooted to the side, and Gavin spread the gray wool blanket where they had been, settling himself on the opposite side of Jewel from Mac and leaning close to whisper, "I think you've already started my fire."

Mac couldn't help overhearing. Or seeing Jewel stiffen slightly before she managed a smile and replied, "Give me a match, and I'll show you a real blaze."

Gavin, damn him, laughed and handed her a box of matches. Instead of letting her light the match by herself, Gavin held her hand as she drew the match along the edge of the box and lit the kindling. When the fire from the match had almost reached her fingers, Gavin lifted her hand to his mouth and blew it out.

Jewel made a mewling sound that had Mac's

insides clenching. His hands fisted uncon-sciously, and his body tensed to fight.

Until that moment, Mac had not realized the extent of his feelings for Jewel. He had always liked her and considered himself her friend. He had missed talking to her in the years they had been apart. He was more than a little attracted to her. But the instinctual need to claim her, to make her his and only his, rose unbidden from somewhere deep inside him.

He resisted the strong urge to hit Gavin Talbot in the nose and began straightening out a clothes hanger to use as a roasting stick. Fighting the metal was a better release for his tension than starting an uncivilized brawl.

It was abundantly clear to him now, as it had not been before, that he wanted to be the man Jewel gave herself to for the first time. He wanted to see her eyes when their bodies were joined, hear her sighs as she learned the pleasure to be found in loving each other.

But Gavin moved fast, and Mac wasn't sure he was going to get a second chance with Jewel if something didn't happen pretty quick to sep-arate the two. It didn't take much of a fire to toast marshmallows, and it wasn't long before Colt opened the bag and began tossing marshmallows around. Gavin was making Jewel laugh again, putting a marshmallow on the end of her roasting stick and whispering in her ear as it toasted on the fire.

"Jewel," Mac said quietly.

To his surprise, she looked immediately at him. "Yes, Mac?"

"Your marshmallow is on fire."

Because she was looking at him, she swung the burning marshmallow in his direction. Mac caught the coat hanger far enough back not to burn himself and blew out the fire. "Hope you like it charred," he said with a smile.

He blew on it to cool it, then pulled the gooey marshmallow off the end of the wire and held it out to her between thumb and forefinger. She leaned forward, her mouth open, and grabbed Mac's wrist as she bit into it. She held on to his wrist while she chewed, waving her hand at her mouth and making noises because the gooey marshmallow was both hot and deliciously sweet.

Then, as though it were the most natural thing in the world, she leaned over and sucked the rest of the marshmallow off of his thumb, licking it clean with her tongue.

Mac stared at her with avid eyes. She could

have no idea what she was doing. By the time she was done with his thumb and had started on his forefinger, his body was strung as tight as a bowstring.

Jewel looked up at him, his forefinger still in her mouth, and caught his gaze with hers. She might not have realized beforehand what effect she was having on him, but he saw she recognized immediately what she had done.

Ever so slowly, she withdrew his forefinger from her mouth, then let go of his wrist. She had to clear her throat to speak. "I forgot to bring along wet wipes," she said. "I figured that was the best way to get rid of the marshmallow."

Mac took the fingers that had been in her mouth and slowly licked off imaginary specks of sugar. "It seems to be all gone."

He watched Jewel swallow hard before Gavin distracted her attention.

"How about sharing this one with me?" Gavin said, putting a hand on her forearm to stake his claim and holding out a perfectly toasted marshmallow.

Mac saw the goose bumps rise on her flesh where Gavin's hand lay. Saw her tentative smile as she turned back to the other man.

"Sure, Gavin," she said. "I'd like that."

She pulled the gooey marshmallow from the wire and ate half of it before Gavin caught her wrist and, with a grin, turned the marshmallow toward himself. Mac watched in helpless fury as Gavin ate the rest of the marshmallow from her hand and licked her fingers clean.

When Gavin started kissing her fingertips, something inside Mac snapped. "That's it!"

"What?" Jewel said, turning bewildered eyes on him.

"Let's go, Jewel." Mac stood and grabbed Jewel's wrist to drag her to her feet. He was surprised when she resisted.

"What's wrong with you, Mac?" she said.

"I think this has gone far enough." He said the words to the counselor, who understand exactly what his problem was.

Gavin rose to his feet, his legs widespread. "I didn't hear the lady complaining about my attentions."

Gavin had a point. But Mac wasn't in a rational mood. "The lady is too polite to say anything."

Gavin raised a questioning brow and faced Jewel. "Is that true, Jewel?"

"I don't see... I mean, I think I may have encouraged... I just wanted to see..."

Gavin's lip curved wryly on one side. "Your point is taken," he said to Mac.

By then, Colt was on his feet on the other side of the fire. "You need any help, Mac?"

Jenny grabbed Colt's T-shirt where it hung out of his jeans and yanked on it. "Sit down, Colt. This doesn't concern you."

"She's my sister."

"Sit down, Colt," Jenny repeated.

Mac watched as Colt met Jenny's gaze and settled back onto the ground beside her.

By then, Jewel was up and standing nose to nose with Mac. "What's gotten into you?" she demanded in a harsh whisper. "You're the one who told me to flirt with him in the first place!"

"I didn't think it would go this far," Mac said stubbornly.

"Thanks to you," she hissed, "it's not likely to go much further!"

"That's fine by me," Mac retorted.

"I think I'll excuse myself and let you two settle this alone," Gavin said. "I can find my own way back."

"We'd better get going, too," Jenny said, rising and pulling Huck and Colt to their feet. "I don't want to be late getting home."

Within moments, everything had been picked

up and repacked, and the four of them were on their way back to the ranch house, leaving Mac and Jewel to put out the fire.

"All right, Mac," Jewel said. "I want to hear from your own lips what possessed you to cause such a scene."

Jewel was confused by Mac's strange behavior. "You're the one who told me to try out my feminine wiles," she said. "The first time I do, you act like a jealous lover."

She thought Mac flushed, but it was hard to tell in the firelight.

"I thought you wanted me along to protect you," he said.

"If I needed protection. Which I did not."

Mac kicked sand over the fire, creating a cloud of smoke. "You *liked* the way he was pawing you?"

"*Pawing* me?" she said. "Gavin's attentions weren't at all unwelcome."

When Gavin had smiled at her, she had allowed herself to feel the pleasure of being attractive to—and attracted to—a handsome man. When he had blown out the match, and his warm, moist breath touched her hand, she had not cut off the frisson of awareness that skittered

down her spine. When he had kissed her fingertips, she had felt her heart beat more rapidly in
response.

But none of those feelings in any way compared to the shock of awareness she felt when
she had met Mac's gaze and discovered he had
been aroused by the way she had sucked and
licked his fingers clean.

It was the difference between a pinprick and
being stabbed with a knife. While she was completely aware of both, one was slight and fleet-
ing, while the other burned deep inside. One
would disappear quickly; the other would not
soon be forgotten.

She wasn't about to admit her vulnerability to
Mac when he was behaving like a jealous idiot.
Especially when he wasn't volunteering to take
Gavin's place. "I liked what Gavin did," she
said.

"I didn't," Mac said flatly.

"Why not?" Jewel demanded.

"He was moving too fast. You hardly know
the guy."

"He didn't do anything I didn't allow."

"That's another thing," Mac said. "Just how
far were you intending to go? Would you have
let him kiss you?"

"Why not?" she said tartly.

Mac made a threatening, rumbly sound in his throat. "I can kiss you as well as some stranger can. If it's kisses you want, come to me."

"Last night you said—"

"Forget about last night. It never happened. We start new, here and now. You want to practice being a woman, practice with me."

Jewel eyed Mac in astonishment. She had exactly what she had thought she wanted. All she had to do was find the courage to follow through and take Mac up on his offer. She took a deep breath, let it out and said, "All right. I'll practice with you."

Mac heaved a sigh and knelt down to stir the ashes with a stick to make certain the fire was out. "Thank God that's settled."

"I want to be kissed, Mac."

She watched his shoulders tense, saw him drop the stick, then rise to face her.

"You want to be kissed now?"

"If you hadn't scared Gavin away, he'd be kissing me now," she pointed out.

It was hard to tell what Mac was feeling. His eyes were narrowed in—anger? His lips were twisted in a moue of—frustration? And his brow was furrowed deep with—apprehension? Which showed how good she was at reading men. What did Mac Macready have to be anxious about? He must have kissed a hundred women. She was the one who needed lessons.

"Come here, Jewel," Mac said in a voice that grated like an unoiled hinge.

It only took a couple of steps for her to reach him. His arms opened wide, and as she stepped between them, they folded around her. One hand caught at her nape, the other low on her spine, just above her buttocks. She was aware of goose bumps rising along her nape as his hand slid up and grasped a handful of her hair.

He did not pull her any closer, simply angled her head and lowered his mouth. His lips felt warm and full as he rubbed them against hers. "Are you sure about this, Jewel?" he breathed against her half-open mouth.

She made a sound in her throat which he must have taken as assent, because he kissed the left side of her mouth, then the right, before returning to the center. He slipped his tongue beneath her upper lip, then nipped at her lips with his teeth.

Jewel shivered. It was strange, standing upright, being held—but not held—in a man's arms. She leaned into the kiss, returning the gentle pressure of his mouth. She slid her tongue along the seam of his lips, and he opened for her. Jewel had never been the aggressor with a man. It felt wonderful to be able to taste and tease to her heart's content without being afraid.

Her arms roamed up Mac's back, feeling the corded sinew. One hand slid into the hair at his nape and played with it as she indulged herself kissing him, feeling the damp softness of his lips, tasting the inside of his mouth with soft, tentative thrusts that he returned. She felt him begin to tremble.

"Jewel," he murmured.

"Hmm." Her lips followed the line of his chin to a spot below his ear, and she heard him hiss in a breath.

"I think we'd better stop."

She leaned back and looked up into his hooded eyes, at lips rigid with passion. She smiled. "If I look anything like you do, perhaps you're right."

"You look beautiful," he said fervently.

"You don't have to say that," Jewel protested. "I know what I—"

He put his mouth on hers to silence her, pouring his feelings into a kiss that had her straining to be closer to him, closing the distance between them, until they were pressed close from breast to thigh. Jewel was so entranced by what Mac was doing with his mouth that it took her a moment to realize he had widened his stance enough to fit her between his legs.

He was aroused.

She squeezed her eyes shut and tried to concentrate on the kiss. It was so lovely. It felt so good. But her body below the waist had turned to stone.

Mac broke the kiss and looked down at her, his eyes worried. "Jewel?"

"Let me go, Mac."

"I won't hurt you, Jewel." He put one hand on her buttocks to keep her where she was. He smiled tenderly. "I'd very much like to put myself inside you."

Jewel felt the heat climbing up her throat at such plain speaking. "Mac—"

"But I'm not going to do anything until you're ready," he said, leaning down to give her a gentle kiss on the lips. "We have plenty of time."

"Your recuperation is almost complete," Jewel countered. "Look how far you've come in—"

He stopped her with another kiss. "We have

plenty of time for you to get used to me touching you, wanting you."

"It doesn't seem fair, Mac. I mean, for me to use you like this."

He smiled. "Believe me, I don't mind."

His eyes seemed to be promising things she knew he could not mean. She looked down and said, "In a couple of weeks you'll be leaving here, and I won't be seeing you again."

He lifted her chin until she was looking into his eyes. "You'll always be special to me, Jewel. You have no idea how special." He opened his mouth as though to say something else and closed it again. "Look, let's just take this one day at a time. You can start with simple stuff like kisses and touches. Anytime you want to practice, just let me know. How does that sound?"

"Are you sure I won't be imposing?" Jewel asked.

"It'll be my pleasure," Mac said with a grin, rocking his body against hers.

"Oh!"

His brow wrinkled in concern. "What's wrong?"

"You're still...and I'm not... It's working!" she said with delight. "I'm hardly affected at all.'' Except that her pulse was throbbing, and she felt the strangest urge to push back against the hardness that rested between her legs.

Mac's smile looked a little forced. "See. You're already getting used to me."

He released her, and Jewel took a step back.

"I suppose we'd better get back," she said. "Camp starts tomorrow, and I'll be getting up early."

"I can help you after my workout."

Jewel smiled. "I'd like that."

"Don't forget. Anytime you feel like you want to practice, just let me know. There's no need to flirt with that Gavin character."

"I thought I might try my wings—"

"Try your wings on me!" He swung her back into his arms, kissed her hard on the lips, then stomped off toward his horse, leaving her standing there.

It took a minute for Jewel to catch her breath and steady her racing pulse. "I was just teasing!" she called after him, as she hurried to catch up.

Mac made a growling sound in his throat. "Let's go. It's late."

She stomped right over and stood in front of

him. "For heaven's sake! Where's your sense of humor?"

He grabbed her hand and placed it on the bulge in his jeans. "Right there. I'm not feeling too damn funny at the moment."

Even though he had immediately let go of her hand, Jewel was too shocked to jerk away. She left her hand where Mac had put it, feeling the length and hardness of him. This part of him didn't seem nearly so threatening through a layer of denim and cotton, warm and pulsing beneath her hand.

"Jewel," he said through gritted teeth. "What are you doing?"

"Learning."

He gave a choked laugh. "I think my sense of humor is—"

"In very fine shape," she said with a gamine grin. "Want to test it again?"

He caught her wrist and removed her hand. "I think I've had enough testing for one evening. Let's save this for another time."

"Anything you say, Mac," she answered cheerfully. "You're the teacher."

And Jewel was determined to be a very good pupil.

Chapter 10

Mac realized the dilemma he had put himself in. He was going to be kissing and touching Jewel over the next several weeks—and encouraging her to kiss and touch him—even though he had serious reservations about making love to her. Not because he didn't desire her, but because he was afraid if he did something wrong, he would mess things up for her even more. He decided he owed it to both of them to get some professional advice.

"Something's come up that I need to discuss with my agent," Mac said to Jewel at breakfast the next morning. "I've made reservations to fly to Dallas this afternoon."

"Couldn't you do it over the phone?" Jewel asked.

Mac shook his head and raised another spoonful of cornflakes. "Too sensitive. Requires face-to-face consultation."

"Why didn't you say something about this last night?" she asked suspiciously.

He grinned. "I was distracted last night."

Jewel blushed. Mac thought she had never looked lovelier. She was wearing a plaid Western shirt, tucked in at the waist of her jeans, that hinted at the fullness of her figure. Her brown hair looked sun kissed, and her brown eyes gleamed. As she turned toward him, the faded crisscross scars on her face took him back to a time when they were both much younger and someone had teased her about them.

Mac realized he must have cared a great deal for her even then. He could remember wiping away her tears with his thumbs, kissing her scarred cheek and saying, "These scars are as precious as any other part of you, Jewel, more facets to add texture to the diamond you are."

He had meant it then, and he could see it now.

Jewel laid her spoon in her cereal bowl and

said, "I'll miss you, Mac. When will you be back?"

Mac met her troubled gaze and said, "I don't know." He had no idea how long it would take to get an appointment with the one sex therapist he knew. Dr. Timothy Douglas might be too busy to fit him in for several days.

"You're not coming back, are you?" Jewel said flatly. "You've changed your mind about wanting to teach me, and you're leaving." The glow had left her face and the sparkle had faded from her eyes.

"What do I have to do to convince you I'm not going away?"

"Kiss me," she said. "That was the deal. I could ask anytime, and I'm asking now." She crossed her arms over her chest as though she thought he might refuse.

Silly woman. He wasn't about to refuse.

Mac crossed to Jewel in two steps, tipped her chin up and slanted his mouth over hers, kissing her with all the passion he felt, hoping to convince her he meant what he said. They were both breathing hard when he lifted his head. "I'm coming back," he said. "I just have some business to do in Dallas."

Tears filled her eyes as she looked up at him. "That was goodbye. I know it."

Mac shook his head in disbelief. He stood and put his hands on his hips. "Look, Jewel. Why would I make an offer like the one I made last night and leave the next day for good?"

"Because you had second thoughts," she said.

"No, I did not."

"Because you realized I might fall in love with you or something stupid like that, if you started kissing me all the time."

"That never crossed my mind!" The thought hadn't occurred to him, but he liked the idea now that she mentioned it.

"Probably you never thought of me falling in love, because kisses don't mean much to a man like you," she said, lips pouting.

How wrong she was! Mac thought. Her kisses, at least, made him feel a great deal, though he wasn't willing to go so far as to think in terms of love. A great deal of *like*. That was what he felt for Jewel Whitelaw.

But he couldn't resist kissing her again. He slipped his tongue inside her mouth and tasted her thoroughly. When he stood again, the revealing bulge was back in his jeans. He noticed that she noticed and felt his body tighten in expectation.

"I'll be back, Jewel. Trust me."

It was a lot to ask a woman who hadn't found much about men to trust.

She blinked back the tears and said, "All right, Mac."

He kissed her again, to thank her for trusting him, but when he felt the urge to pull her up and into his arms, he stepped back. "You've got campers to see to, and I've got a few things to do before I join you."

"You're still going to help me with the campers this morning?"

"Of course. Why wouldn't I?"

"I thought you might have to pack..."

"I'm only taking a few things."

She walked back to him and put her arms around him and hugged him tight. "I'm so glad you're coming back," she said. "I'll be waiting for you. I won't even flirt with Gavin while you're gone."

She was already halfway to the door by the time he realized what she had said. She turned back, winked and laughed, then headed out the door.

Mac watched her till she was gone, realizing

he had more problems to solve than just hers, if they were to have any hope of a future together. He had gotten a big signing bonus when he joined the Tornadoes, but his five-year contract had provided for a smaller salary in the first few years. He had most of the signing bonus left, but he had pretty much spent his first year's salary.

What if he didn't make it back onto the team?

Don't even think *that!*

Mac didn't believe in quitting or giving up or giving in. But it was time for a reality check. He had accomplished more than most men would have. He was walking—hell, he was running again—when the doctors said he'd be in a leg brace the rest of his life. He should quit while he was ahead. If he went back to playing football, chances were good he'd reinjure his leg. Maybe next time his prognosis would be even worse.

Mac called his agent's office and got Andy's secretary. "Tell Andy I'll be in his office about four o'clock this afternoon. I'll fill him in on everything when I see him."

He headed out the door dressed in a starched white oxford-cloth shirt belted into crisp new jeans and almost new ostrich cowboy boots, so he'd be ready if the media caught sight of him in Dallas. Mac wanted to look confident and ready to go back to work for the Tornadoes on the outside, even if he didn't feel quite that way inside.

He stopped at the boys' bunkhouse to check on Brad Templeton, but apparently the kids had already headed over to the cookhouse for breakfast. He was about to leave when he heard something hit the tile floor in the communal bathroom. He stepped inside. "Who's there?"

Nobody answered, but Mac knocked on the frame of the open bathroom doorway and said, "Anybody here?"

Brad Templeton stepped out of one of the four shower-curtained stalls. "How'd you know I was here?"

"I heard something drop."

He made a face. "My plastic cup."

"Why aren't you at breakfast with the other kids?" Mac asked, leaning casually against the bathroom doorway to put the kid at ease.

"I told Gavin I didn't feel well."

Mac's easy pose evaporated. He took the few steps to bring him to Brad's side, whipped off the kid's New York Mets baseball cap and pressed his hand on Brad's forehead. It all happened so fast, Brad didn't have a chance to complain until Mac had already found out what he wanted to know. He replaced the cap. "No fever," he said.

Brad tugged the ball cap back down over his nearly bald head. "Naw. I'm okay."

Fever was one of the first—and worst—signs that a remission was over, that the leukemia was back. It wasn't something to be ignored. "Why'd you tell Gavin you were sick?" Mac asked.

Brad shrugged, the kind of kid gesture that could have meant anything, but really meant, *I couldn't tell him the truth.*

"What's on the agenda this morning?" Mac asked.

"Horseback riding," Brad mumbled.

"That sounds like fun. What's the problem?"

"I've never been on a horse before. I'd probably get bucked off and stomped to death. I don't want to die any sooner than I have to."

Mac grinned.

"That's not funny!" Brad said.

"You sound exactly like I did when I went riding the first time. Funny how being sick makes you want to live all the more, isn't it?"

Brad's brows rose almost to the brim of his ball cap. It was one thing for Mac to say he'd been sick, another for him to express a feeling that could only be had by someone who had personally faced death.

"Come on," Mac said, putting a hand on Brad's shoulder and ushering him toward the door. "Let's get you fed. I know just the pony for you. Gentle as a lamb."

"What's his name?" Brad asked.

Mac grinned. "Buttercup."

Mac paced the confines of Andy Dennison's office, from the bat signed by Ken Griffey, Jr., in one corner, to the football signed by Joe Montana in the other and back again. His agent had become his friend, and now he needed some friendly advice. But Andy was late.

He had too much time to think.

Andy must have leaked what time Mac was landing at Dallas/Fort Worth International Airport, because a bunch of photographers and reporters had been waiting for him when he exited the jetway. He had smiled for the cameras as he walked quickly toward the chauffeur-driven limousine waiting for him outside.

"It's great to see you walking so well, Mac," one reporter commented. "Will you be back with the Tornadoes this fall?"

"That's my plan," Mac said.

"You can walk. But can you run?" another reporter asked.

Mac smiled more broadly. "Does a Texas dog have fleas?"

Everybody laughed, but the reporter persisted. "What's your time for the forty?"

Mac's time for the forty-yard dash wasn't anywhere near the four-point-something-second range of most wide receivers, and nothing close to his own previous time. His hesitation in answering hinted at the problems he was having, and the reporters, smelling blood, attacked in earnest.

"Have you come to Dallas to announce your retirement?" one speculated.

"No," Mac said flatly.

"Are you here to see a doctor about your leg?"

"No."

"Are you negotiating with the Tornadoes to get your spot on the team back?"

"No comment."

That gave them more meat to chew on and distracted them from other lines of questioning. They asked a dozen more questions aimed at determining his exact status with the Tornadoes, before he reached the limousine and safety.

"Remind me to kill Andy when I see him," he muttered to Andy's driver.

The old man laughed. "He thought you could use the publicity."

"Why wasn't he here to keep the wolves off of me?"

"He's working on a big deal. Said he'd see you at the office at four, like you asked. You're all set up to stay at the Wyndham Hotel. I can take you there to freshen up, if you'd like."

"I need to make another stop first." Mac gave Andy's chauffeur the address of the sex therapist, who had agreed to see him today during a time someone else had canceled an appointment.

Dr. Timothy Douglas had first talked to Mac in the hospital after one of his operations, when Mac was scared to death that he would be impotent for life because nothing seemed to be working. The doctor had reassured Mac that the medication he was taking—and his state of agitation over the problem—had caused his lack of sex drive.

Douglas was not much older than Mac, but he was balding and wore spectacles, both of which made him look more distinguished. The good doctor had returned several times over the years to talk to Mac in the hospital, and it was during one of those discussions that Mac had admitted he was a virgin.

Douglas hadn't been able to control a smile. "Good for you," he'd said. "Too many men are indiscriminate these days."

"Sorry to burst your bubble, Doc, but I doubt I'd be able to say that if I'd been out of this bed more than a day at a time over the past couple of years."

Douglas patted his shoulder and said, "Wait for the right woman, Mac. You won't be sorry."

Douglas was the only person in the world who knew Mac's secret. And the only one he felt comfortable telling about Jewel's secret. Surely the good doctor could come up with some suggestions for how Mac could help Jewel without hurting her.

"This is a doctor's office," the chauffeur said when he stopped in front of the address Mac had given him.

"Sure is," Mac said. "Meet me back here in an hour."

Mac let himself out of the sleek black car and headed inside the office building.

The hour Mac spent with Timothy Douglas

had been well worth the time and trouble to get there. As he paced his agent's office, Mac worked through the various suggestions Douglas had made for how he could help Jewel.

"Patience is essential," Douglas said. "Thoughtfulness. Consideration. All the things you would normally expect in a loving relationship. Only, each step of the way, you need to check with Jewel to make sure she's still with you. Understand?"

Mac understood all right. The man was supposed to control himself while he attended to the woman first. "What if I can't wait?" he blurted, his face crimson with embarrassment.

"Do you care for this woman?" Douglas asked.

"Why the hell do you think I'm so worried?" Mac shot back. "What if I lose control and make things worse?"

"Be sure you're thinking of her at the crucial moment, instead of yourself, and everything will turn out fine."

"That's all there is to it?" Mac asked skeptically.

"Sex is a natural bodily function," Douglas said. "We're supposed to procreate. Your body will know what to do, even if you don't."

Mac took comfort in that last word of advice. But as he was very well aware, knowing technically what to do, and actually doing it, sometimes turned out to be two entirely different things.

On Mac's next lap across his agent's office, the door opened and Andy Dennison stepped inside.

"Hi there, Mac. What's new?"

"I can walk. And I can run."

Andy smiled and crossed to shake Mac's hand. "Congratulations. I should have known you would do what you promised. How about a cigar to celebrate?"

"No thanks," Mac said with a smile. "I'm in training."

"You don't mind if I have one." Andy crossed to his desk, took a cigar from a box on top of it, clipped the end with a sterling silver device, sniffed it and rolled the tobacco lovingly between his fingers. That was as far as he could go. No smoking was allowed in the building.

"When can I set up an appointment with the Tornadoes?" Andy asked.

"Not so fast," Mac said, seating himself in one of the two modern chrome and black leather chairs facing the desk. "What's the last date I could show up in training camp and still have a chance to make the team?"

"Depends on how fast you can run when you show up," Andy said bluntly.

"How fast is the new kid?"

Andy gave Mac a figure for the forty that made sweat bead on Mac's forehead. It was two seconds better than Mac's best time before he was injured.

"What about his hands?"

"Misses a few. Fumbles now and again."

Mac smiled. "Then I have a chance. Being fastest isn't everything. I proved that when I played."

"Yeah. But being slow will get you cut from the team," Andy pointed out.

"How slow is too slow?" Mac asked, leaning forward, his elbows on his knees.

Andy shrugged. "Hard to say. But if you aren't within a second or two of your best time..." Andy shrugged again.

Mac sighed and sat back, crossing his good ankle over his scarred knee. "I was afraid of that."

"Look, there's been some interest in using you as a sports commentator. Why not let me follow up and—"

"That isn't what I want to do with my life."

"What are you planning to do? I mean, if you don't make the team?"

Mac drew a complete blank. "I don't know. I haven't thought about it much."

"Maybe you should," Andy said. "Think about that sportscasting job. It's national television, lots of exposure, possibility of advertising bucks. Lot of dough in a job like that."

"Lots of travel, too," Mac said.

"Yeah, there's that."

"I want to settle down somewhere and have a family."

Andy cleared his throat. "Uh. I heard about that stop you made this afternoon. Anything I can do to help?"

Mac laughed. "It's taken care of, but thanks for the offer."

"Sure, Mac, just know I'm there if you need me. By the way, who's the girl?"

"Knowing your penchant for publicity I figure I'll keep that to myself for a while."

"Hey. Whatever you want," Andy said. "By the way, how long are you going to be in town?"

"Just overnight."

"Anxious to get back to your girl?" Andy said with a sly smile.

Mac thought about it, smiled and answered, "Yeah. I am."

"Look, I know some folks who'd like to have dinner with you. How about it?"

"Will it help you out?"

Andy grinned. "You're a great guy, Mac. I knew you'd come through. I'll have a tux delivered to your hotel room, and I'll have my limo pick you up at eight."

"A tux! What kind of shindig is this?"

"Charity ball in Forth Worth, complete with politicians and socialites. Won't hurt you to be seen there, Mac. You can use all the good press you can get. You'll be sitting at the mayor's table."

Mac shook his head. "How do I let you talk me into these things?"

Andy stuck the cigar between his teeth and grinned. "You like me?"

Instead of laughing, Mac looked Andy in the eye and said, "You stuck with me when a lot of other folks didn't. I'm not likely to forget that anytime soon." He left before Andy could form a response.

Chapter 11

Colt sat on the sagging back porch of Jenny's house waiting for Huck to come back out. He tugged at the frayed knee of his jeans, making the tear worse, then glanced up at the hot, noonday sun. He couldn't get what Mac had said about Huck and Jenny out of his mind.

College is a long way off. Maybe they'll change their minds about each other.

Colt would never do anything to separate the two of them—not that he believed anything could alter Jenny's devotion to Huck—but Mac had offered him a sort of hope he hadn't allowed himself to feel in a very long time.

Lately, Colt let his eyes linger on her more. He let his heart fall more completely under her spell. Even though his head said it was a stupid thing to do.

"Hey, Colt. You ready to go?"

Colt leapt up guiltily as the kitchen screen door slammed and stuck his hands deep into his back pockets. "Yeah. Sure." *Good thing Huck couldn't read his mind.*

"You're acting awful jumpy lately. What's your problem?" Huck asked as he crossed past Colt and down the creaking steps. "Some girl finally caught your eye?" he teased.

Maybe Huck could read minds, Colt thought uncomfortably.

"Who is it? Sarah Logan? Freda Barnett? I know—Betty Lou Tucker!"

Betty Lou Tucker was the prettiest—and most curvaceous—girl in school. Huck was way off the mark. The only girl Colt ever thought about was Jenny. And Jenny wasn't beautiful, she was just…Jenny. Colt thought of Jenny looking up at him with her bluer-than-blue eyes and felt the heat rising up his throat to make visible spots on his cheeks.

"Thought so," Huck said with a laugh. "Betty Lou's been looking at a lot of guys since she broke up with Bobby Ray.'' Huck unlooped the reins from the tie rail in front of the Double D ranch house and mounted his horse. ''You coming with me, or you gonna sit on Jenny's back porch all day?''

''I...uh...think I'll wait to talk to Jenny before I leave...about some stuff.''

Huck shook his head in disgust. ''Jenny's gotta feed the little ones before she can do anything. You might be waiting a while. She was asking me if I could help her out, but I've got better things to do with my time than housework. You're welcome to take my place.''

''Maybe I'll do that,'' Colt said, his heart thumping a little harder.

''See you tonight at the movies?'' Huck asked.

''Naw. My dad asked me to do some bookkeeping with him.''

''When are you gonna tell him you're not gonna stay on the ranch?'' Huck asked.

''Sometime,'' Colt said.

''Better be soon, or he'll be depending on you so much you'll never get out,'' Huck warned.

''I hear you,'' Colt said irritably.

Huck kicked his horse into a lope, raising a

choking cloud of dust from the dry, sunbaked dirt around the house.

Colt stepped back and waved away the worst of it so he could breathe, then turned and stared at the screen door. All he had to do was knock and offer his help. It was bound to seem a little odd to Jenny for him to volunteer, since he'd never been in her house before.

There was a reason for that. He stayed away from sick people, and her mother had been sick nearly the whole time he'd known her. Her mother's breast cancer had gone into remission for a long time, but after the youngest child was born, it had come back.

Now Mrs. Wright was dying of cancer. Colt knew what that meant. Hair falling out from chemotherapy. Frail limbs. Eyes dead long before the body was. He had seen too much of it at Camp LittleHawk. Enough to know that it hurt desperately to like—let alone love—someone who was ill and who might or might not survive another week, another month, another year.

The only thing that could make him go inside Jenny's house right now was the knowledge that he would get to spend time alone with her. They would probably talk and maybe laugh together.

That possibility was worth having to share Jenny's pain as she tended to her dying mother.

But Huck had said Jenny was feeding the little ones. Colt was the baby in his family, but he figured he could probably manage whatever Jenny asked of him.

Colt knocked on the door, said, "Jenny, I'm coming in," and let himself inside. He immediately took off his Western straw hat and stood still inside the screen door until his eyes adjusted to the darker room. When he could see, he found Jenny staring at him, her jaw hanging open.

"Colt. What are you doing in here?"

"Huck thought you might need some help." He clutched the hat against his chest feeling foolish, but said, "Here I am."

She smiled, and he knew it was going to be all right. He looked for a place to hang his hat, but didn't see anything.

"Put it on top of the refrigerator," she said. "That way Tyler and James can't get to it."

He looked at the baby sitting in the high chair before her and the older child sitting in a youth chair next to him. "They seem pretty well lassoed," he said, but he put the hat where she told him, anyway.

She gestured him toward her. "This is

Randy," she said, sticking another spoonful of something gross looking in the baby's mouth, "and next to him is Sam. Tyler and James are playing in their room.

"Here. You can take my place." She rose and handed Colt the baby spoon and the open jar of baby food. "Randy loves peas."

Colt took one look at the contents of the jar and nearly gagged. "This doesn't look edible."

Jenny laughed, and he felt his whole body go still at the sound. "Don't tell Randy. He eats it like it was green ice cream."

Colt sat in the chair she had vacated and aimed a spoon of peas in Randy's direction. When his mouth opened, Colt shoved it in, and Randy cleaned it off. "He's a human vacuum cleaner!"

"He'll probably end up as big and tall as my dad," Jenny said as she set a plate of more recognizable food in front of Sam. The music had gone out of her voice by the time she got to the end of her sentence.

"Where is your dad?"

"He left," she said, her eyes focused on Sam. "Took off when Mom got sick the second time."

"I'm sorry, Jenny. I didn't know."

She tried to make light of it. "Can't really blame him. It isn't pretty to watch someone die. He loved her very much, you know."

Colt couldn't believe how matter-of-factly she was speaking about such a tragic situation. "It must be hard for you and your mom to get along on your own."

Her chin came up, and she looked at him with her incredible blue eyes. "We manage."

He heard her message loud and clear: *Don't feel sorry for me.* He admired her gumption. But what choice did she have? She wasn't old enough to leave home and get a job. Where would she go? He realized now why she had been so worried about being left behind by Huck.

"Good thing you have so much help around the house," he said. "All those brothers, I mean."

"I'm the eldest," she said. "Tyler is ten, James is nine, Sam is five and Randy will be one in a couple of months."

"Who takes care of them when you're in school?"

"Mom has a sister who takes care of her during the days and keeps an eye on the little ones.

I pick up the slack at night and give Aunt Lenore a rest.''

Colt caught her glance for a moment and saw a sort of desperation he had often felt himself. A yearning to be free to follow your own path, to see the world, to explore to your heart's content. And the knowledge that destiny—or your parents or family—had other plans for you.

He had thought Huck was the only impediment to having Jenny. He saw now what the future held for her as well as she probably saw it herself. Unless she ran away, and he did not see Jenny as the kind of person who ran away from anything, she would be tied to her family until the boys were grown.

Huck would leave her behind when she couldn't go with him, because Huck would never understand why she couldn't go. Colt understood, though. It was the same reason he might never fly jets. Because she couldn't bear to hurt her family to please herself. As he could never bear to hurt his.

Colt wanted to tell her that he understood. That he knew what she faced. That he would be there for her, even if Huck wasn't.

What if you get a chance to fly jets? an inner

voice asked. *Would you stay and work at Hawk's Pride just to be near Jenny?*

Colt was glad he didn't have to make that kind of decision for four years. He would be here for her now. Even though she was Huck's girl. And might always be.

Jewel, Patty and Gavin were sitting in the sand at the bottom of a canyon with eleven campers, pencils and notepads in hand, sketching the primitive art etched on the stone canyon wall that rose up on one side of them.

Some of the kids were sitting cross-legged, some lay on their stomachs. Only one child had not relaxed and made himself comfortable. The twelfth camper, Brad Templeton, stood directly in front of the wall, staring up at it intently.

"How are you doing?" Jewel asked the campers as she rose and began to walk among them to see what they had produced in the half hour they had been drawing.

"Okay."

"Pretty good."

"What's that thing there?" A girl's finger pointed to a stick horse etched on the stone wall.

"What does it look like?" Jewel asked.

"It's a horse, dummy," the boy sitting next to the girl said scornfully.

"Yes, it is, Louis," Jewel said. "But you can see why Nolie might not recognize it. It could be some other animal."

"It has a long tail and pointy ears like a horse," Louis said.

"True. But some dogs have long tails and pointy ears."

"Oh," Louis said thoughtfully. "It looked like a horse to me."

"That's why we're making these drawings," Jewel explained. "And writing down what we think they mean." She put a supportive hand on Patty's shoulder as she encouraged one of the campers and exchanged a thankful look with Gavin, who had one of the youngest—and most homesick—campers sitting in his lap.

"We'll send your drawings to an archaeologist at the university who studies primitive art. She can tell us what she thinks the drawing means. When I send you her findings later this summer, you can compare your conclusions with hers."

"Does the drawing really mean something?" another little girl asked, staring at the primitive figures.

Jewel shrugged and smiled. "I don't know. Maybe someone a long time ago was just having fun drawing."

The kids laughed.

Jewel had reached Brad's side and noticed his drawing pad was blank. "Is something wrong, Brad?" she asked quietly.

He kept his eyes on the stone wall and spoke in a voice that only she could hear. "I know what it means," he said.

"You do?" Jewel turned to stare at the wall of stick figures and arrows pointing in different directions with a sun above it all. "Tell me. I've always been curious."

"What does it matter? What does anything matter?"

Jewel's brow furrowed. "You can't give up, Brad," she said.

"Why not?" he shot back. "People give up on stuff all the time. They quit hobbies and they quit school and they quit jobs."

"They don't quit living," she said.

"Some do," he said stubbornly. "They just stop doing things. You know what I mean."

Jewel felt a chill run down her spine. *People like her. As afraid of living as Brad was of dying.* "Tell me about the drawings, Brad."

He turned to look up at the wall. "The man wants to go somewhere far away, to have an adventure. But he isn't sure which is the best way to go. So he doesn't go anywhere at all. He stays right where he is. Where it's safe."

Jewel stared at the wall. The sun shone brightly above a stick-figure man and his stick-figure horse. They were surrounded by arrows pointing in all different directions—some of them back at the man himself.

He doesn't go anywhere at all. He stays right where he is. Where it's safe.

Jewel's throat squeezed closed. Brad might have been describing her own life for the past six years. Recently she had begun to make changes, but even so, she had been relying on Mac to get her over the worst hurdles. That had to stop. She had to start thinking about moving forward on her own. Or she might end up stuck forever right where she was.

She had to stop letting the past control her present. She had to open herself to new relationships. She couldn't count on Mac to solve her problems. He wanted to be her friend, nothing more. That had become apparent when she discovered from reading the newspapers the real reason he had gone to Dallas three days ago.

She had died a little inside when she opened the Dallas newspaper the day after Mac had left and found a picture of Mac and Eve Latham smiling at each other at a Fort Worth charity function. If Eve was the woman Mac wanted, Jewel had to accept that and move on. She had to find the courage to start living again—without Mac's help.

The same way Brad had to keep on living, despite the fact he might be dying. "Do you think he ever took the trip?" Jewel asked softly.

Brad shook his head, and a tear spilled on his cheek. He knuckled it away with his fist. "He waited too late," Brad whispered.

Jewel took a step closer and enfolded Brad in her arms. Her chin quivered, and she gritted her teeth to keep from making any sound. How could she have been working here all these years and not have seen what Brad could see so clearly? How could she have let so many years go by not living life when it was so precious? How could she have given fear such a stranglehold on her future?

"It's never too late, Brad," she said fiercely. "All you have to do is take that first step, and then another, and another." She rubbed his shoulders soothingly, then pushed him back and tipped up his chin so she could see his eyes beneath the baseball cap. "Just one step, Brad. And the adventure begins."

"Everything all right here?" Gavin had brought the homesick child with him in his arms.

Jewel swallowed back the knot in her throat and turned to Gavin with a smile. "Sure. I think Brad is ready to do some drawing. Right, Brad?"

"Yeah," he mumbled.

"This one is about ready to go back," Gavin said, gesturing to the little girl with his chin. She looked happy and comfortable in Gavin's arms. He really was a great guy, Jewel thought, just not the guy for her.

"Tell you what," Jewel said. "Why don't you and Patty gather up everyone else and get them started back. I'll stay here a little while longer with Brad."

"You sure?" Gavin asked doubtfully. "It's pretty isolated out here."

Jewel laughed. "Hawk's Pride is safer than most big cities. Brad and I will be fine."

"Okay," Gavin said with a smile. "See you later."

"Thanks, Gavin."

"You're welcome, Boss," he said over his

shoulder. "Come on, guys. Let's get you all mounted up," he called to the campers. "Day's wastin'."

Jewel helped Gavin and Patty make sure all the campers were comfortable for the horseback ride up out of the canyon. Then she crossed back to where Brad was industriously working on his drawing.

"That's looking pretty good," Jewel said, admiring his sketch.

"I've had a lot of time to practice," Brad said, his lips curling wryly.

"What do you want to be when you grow up?" Jewel asked.

"I wanted to be a football player," Brad said, changing it to the past tense. "Like Mac Macready."

"Let's get some practice, then," Mac said.

Jewel and Brad both jerked their heads toward the sound of Mac's voice. He dismounted from his horse, a football tucked into his elbow.

Jewel was surprised Mac had returned, especially after seeing the photo of him with his arm around Eve Latham. Her first impulse was to rail at him, but she had no claims on Mac Macready. What "business" he did in his free time was up to him. She just wished he hadn't lied to her

about why he had gone to Dallas. That wasn't
something friends did to friends.

"What are you doing here?" Jewel said, her
voice sharp despite her wish to keep it level.

"I brought a football, figuring I'd throw a few
passes to the kids, but I passed them on the way
down, headed back for lunch. Gavin told me
you'd stayed behind with Brad, so I thought I'd
join you."

"Hi, Mac," Brad said shyly.

"Hi, Brad," Mac said, tossing him the football. "I need to talk with Jewel for a minute.
Why don't you go find us a place where you can
throw me a few?"

"You want me to throw to you?"

"You want to be a football player someday,
don't you? No time like the present to start prac-
ticing."

Brad shot Jewel a questioning look. *Should I
let myself hope? Should I take him up on his
offer?*

"One step, Brad," she said softly. "And the
adventure begins."

The boy smiled broadly and turned back to
Mac. "Okay, Mac. I'll go find us a good spot."
He turned and headed on the run toward a sandy

stretch that extended around a curve in the canyon wall.

Jewel compared the Mac in the newspaper photo to the Mac standing before her. He had looked impressively handsome in a tuxedo. But he was just as impressive dressed in a cutoff T-shirt that showed off a washboard midriff and rippling biceps. Cutoff jeans revealed his scarred leg, but emphasized his height. Tennis shoes and a Texas Rangers baseball cap with his blond hair sticking out every whichaway made him look like one of the kids.

She was quite aware he was not.

Jewel forced herself to stand still as Mac eyed her up and down in return. She was wearing a T-shirt with the neck cut out that was also cut off at midriff, exposing her narrow waist, and very short, fringed cutoffs that showed off her long legs. She might as well have been naked. The look in his eyes made her skin feel prickly all over.

Now that he was back, his gaze seemed to say, they could pick up where they had left off, kissing and touching.

But she could not forget the possessive look in Eve's eyes, or the way Mac's arm reached snugly around her. She was very well aware of how long he had been gone and who he had been with, but she couldn't very well confront him with Brad nearby.

"I missed you," he said softly.

"From the picture in the newspaper I wouldn't have said you were too lonely."

He frowned. "What picture?"

"The one of you with your arm around Eve Latham at a charity ball."

Mac groaned. "I can explain—"

"Later," she said, turning to walk away from him. "Brad is waiting for you."

He caught her arm. "I want this cleared up now. It was nothing, Jewel. Publicity my agent set up."

"With Eve Latham?" she said, raising a doubtful brow.

"With her father, actually. He's a big fan of the Tornadoes."

"I suppose Eve just happened to be there?"

"Believe me, I didn't set that up. In fact, I'd planned to come right back the next morning, but Eve's father arranged a golf game the next morning with the manager of the Tornadoes that I couldn't very well get out of, and my agent snuck a few more appearances into the mix. Believe me, I only wanted to get back here as quickly as I could.''

"Why?" she said, staring him in the eye. "So you could throw footballs to adoring campers?"

For the first time he looked angry. "You know better," he said through clenched teeth.

"Do I? I have no claim on you, Mac. If you'd rather not follow through on what you promised, all you have to do is say so. It isn't necessary to make excuses."

An instant later, he was kissing her hard on the mouth. It was as much a kiss of anger as of passion. Jewel felt both angry and passionate in return. Mac let her go abruptly, his breathing erratic, and said, "I have no intention of backing out on my promise to you. It's up to you whether you choose to take advantage of my offer."

Jewel stared at Mac, appalled at how easily he had aroused her, how easily he had made her want him. She was afraid to let Mac back in. "I thought you'd lied to me about why you went to Dallas," she admitted.

"I would never lie to you, Jewel. That's not something friends do."

She wanted to believe him. She wanted to go back to trusting him. Fear made her cautious. Fear made her reluctant to let him back into her life. Fear could keep her stuck in the same rut forever.

Jewel glanced at the etching on the stone wall. She took a deep breath and let it out. "All right, Mac. You've got yourself a deal."

She held out her hand for him to shake, and Mac raised it to his mouth, kissing it like a courtier of old. His grin reappeared, and she felt her insides flip-flop.

"Very well, my little hyacinth," he said.

"That's a flower."

"And a precious stone," he assured her. "See you in a little while." He let go of her and loped across the sand, calling out to Brad to throw him the ball.

Jewel stared at her hand where Mac had kissed it, then raised her fingertips to her recently kissed lips. Mac had plainly thrown down the gauntlet. She had a chance to grab for life with both hands. She had a chance to practice kissing and touching with him. And she had a chance to explore a relationship with him beyond the friendship they had shared for so many years. She could take it, or reject it. The choice was hers.

What she must not do was make no choice at all.

If she hadn't spent the past half hour in Brad Templeton's company, she might have chickened out. But Jewel couldn't very well demand Brad reach out for life, if she wasn't going to do it herself.

Brad threw Mac the ball and came racing back to her holding out his notepad and pencil.

Jewel exchanged a glance with Mac that was the closest she had ever come to flirting with him. It promised everything…later. She was rewarded with a look that made her body curl inside and her breasts feel achy and swollen.

Jewel felt a tug on her T-shirt and looked down at Brad, who stood beside her again, his eyes gleaming with delight. Oh, yes. Football. And hope.

"I'll take those things," she said, reaching out for Brad's notepad and pencil.

Brad turned and trotted right back to Mac. She saw the boy swallow hard as he reached out for the football Mac was handing him. Jewel thanked Mac with her eyes and got a wink that flustered her in return.

She knew better than to tell either male not to overdo it. But Jewel was concerned as the sun rose higher and Brad continued to throw the ball and Mac continued to run for it. They were both drenched with sweat. Brad looked flushed. And Mac was starting to limp.

"Hey, you two. How about a break?"

She caught Mac's eye and gave him a warning look. He glanced at Brad and said, "I'm whipped, partner. How about a tall, cold glass? Of water, that is," he said, slapping Brad on the shoulder as they started back toward where Jewel sat in the shade of the canyon wall.

Jewel stood up with the canteens ready and handed one to each of them. She lifted Brad's hat as though to rearrange it on his head and surreptitiously checked for a fever. He seemed warm, but the sun was hot. "How are you feeling?" she asked, unable to keep the concern from her voice.

"Fantastic," Brad said, grinning for the first time since he had arrived at camp. "That was fun, Mac. Thanks."

"Tell you what I'm going to do, partner. I'm going to autograph this football to you with thanks for a strong throwing arm, so you can take it home with you."

"Wow! That would be neat," Brad said, sounding more like a kid his age every minute. He flopped down onto the sand, looking exhausted but happy.

Jewel was aware of Mac's wince as he settled onto the ground beside Brad.

"I've got some snacks that'll keep us until we can get some lunch," she said, dropping to her knees and opening what was left of the graham crackers and peanut butter and celery she had brought for the campers. "That'll also give you two a chance to cool off before we make the ride home."

As they munched, Mac and Brad talked. Jewel watched them closely. Brad had a smile on his face and talked a mile a minute, as though someone had turned up the rpms on a record. Mac listened. He didn't look at her often, but often enough to remind her that he was ready and willing whenever she wanted to take that final leap of faith. "Are you ready to head back now?" Jewel asked, when Brad had wound down a little.

"I guess," Brad said. "Can we do this again?" he asked Mac as he shoved himself to his feet.

"As often as you want before you leave," Mac said.

Jewel noticed Mac wincing again as he straightened his scarred leg.

He caught her watching him and grinned, as

though he hadn't just been in pain. "Don't worry. Everything important is working just fine." He leered at her, making it clear exactly what he meant.

Jewel felt flustered and excited. And anxious. Mac looked exhausted. He was using humor—and sexual tension—to distract her and doing a pretty good job. She was also concerned about Brad. He seemed awfully red-faced even after his rest. "Are you sure you're both feeling all right?" she asked.

"I'm doing great!" Brad said.

"I'm just fine," Mac said.

Jewel pursed her lips. Typical males. Everything was fine until they keeled over. She decided to keep a close eye on both of them.

Mac was still grinning as he ushered Brad past her and headed for the horses, whispering for her ears only, "You look beautiful, Amethyst. And very, very desirable. I can't wait for...later."

Jewel's heart started to pound as she stared at Mac's back, wondering if she would have the courage to do this evening what she had been waiting six years to do. His calling her "Amethyst" reminded her that they had been friends for a very long time. That he would never hurt her. That she could trust him.

Surely Brad's admonition about postponing life had made a difference. Surely she would be able to let go of the fear and move forward with her life. All she had to do was take one step. And the adventure would begin.

Chapter 12

Brad was a different child when he entered the cookhouse for lunch—happy, talkative, showing off his football to the other kids and stuffing down a plateful of lasagna as though it was the best meal he had ever eaten. Jewel was proud of Brad for reaching out with both hands toward the future and grateful to Mac for putting an ear-to-ear smile on the boy's face.

However, Mac had not joined them for lunch, pleading the need for a shower. The entire time Jewel ate, she could not get the image of him naked in the shower out of her mind. She had the craziest urge to join him there which, of course, she did not indulge.

After lunch, when the campers took a rest break in their cottages, Jewel had no excuse to linger in the cookhouse. She drew herself up from the bench where she had been sitting and headed toward her cottage, not sure whether she wanted Mac to be out of the shower or not.

When she entered the cottage she felt disappointed not to hear the shower running. There was her answer. She had wanted an excuse to see all of Mac and had been thwarted. She headed for the bathroom anyway, thinking it would be nice to take a quick, cool shower herself while the campers were napping. The bathroom door was open on her side, so she assumed the room was empty.

It was not.

Mac sat in the tub covered with white bubbles—which she presumed had come from the glass-stoppered container of bubble bath she kept on the edge of the tub. He was leaning forward, his teeth gritted, his hands apparently gripping his scarred leg.

"Mac?"

He whipped his head around, swore, then

groaned. She saw his biceps ripple as he applied tremendous pressure to his leg.

"What is it?" she asked. "What's wrong?"

"Cramp," he gritted through his teeth.

She dropped to her knees on the fluffy bath mat beside the tub, her eyes focused on his straining face. "What can I do? How can I help?"

"I can't move...can't get out of the damned tub!"

"Do you want me to help you stand up?"

He shook his head violently and groaned again.

"How long has the muscle been cramped?" she asked.

"Too long," he snapped back.

His face was blanched with pain. The sweat on his brow and above his lip, which she at first thought had to be from the heat of the water, was apparently the result of fighting the cramp. For how long? Fifteen minutes? Twenty? "I'll call 911," she said, pushing off from the tub to stand up.

"Don't! I don't want news of this getting out."

"You need help, Mac," she said, angry because she was frightened.

"Then help me, damn it!"

"How?"

"Maybe two sets of hands working on the muscle will get it to uncramp more quickly."

She hesitated only a moment before dropping back down onto the bath mat. Before she could change her mind, she stuck her hands beneath the thin layer of bubbles into the water—which was merely lukewarm—and reached for his leg. Her hands tangled with his before she moved them upward, closer to his knee.

As she worked her fingers into the tightly clenched calf muscle she asked, "Has this happened before?"

He nodded. "Never this bad." His head rolled back and she watched his jaw muscles work as he struggled to endure the pain without making a sound.

"Please let me call someone, Mac."

"No," he grated out.

"Then let me run some more hot water. Wouldn't that help?"

He met her gaze, struggled with the decision, then nodded.

She tipped the lever to empty the tub, realizing after she did so, that the bubbles were going to run out with the water, leaving Mac exposed.

But she couldn't worry about his modesty—or hers—right now. She was too worried about his pain and the ramifications of Mac having such severe cramps in his leg after what would have been a very light workout if he had really been playing football.

The water drained quickly, and a slurping sound announced the tub was empty. Jewel shot the lever closed and turned on the water, making it as hot as she thought he could stand.

"Too hot?" she asked, turning to look at him for the first time since the tub had begun draining.

"No. It feels good."

Her breath caught at the sight of him covered here and there with bubbles. She quickly turned her head away, but the image of him, wet curls caught on his nape, water pearled on his shoulders, bubbles caught in the curls on his chest—and on other curls—stayed with her.

But not for long. For the first time, she took a good look at the leg she was massaging. "Mac, there's not much muscle left here. It's all scar tissue."

"I know," he said with a discouraged sigh. "That's the problem. What muscle there is left isn't enough to—" His hands gripped his ankle as an agonized cry tore from his throat. She moved her hands near his at the back of his ankle and felt the muscle spasming. The steaming hot water covered their hands as she held on tight with him for the sixty-five long seconds it took the spasm to pass. Suddenly, she felt the entire muscle ease.

Mac hissed out a breath and, after waiting to see if the tension would return, cautiously let go of his leg.

Jewel turned to look at him and saw his face was turned toward the tile wall. And that tears streamed from his eyes. "Oh, Mac."

"Go away, Jewel," he grated out.

She couldn't do that. Not with what she knew now.

Mac's football career was over. He knew it. And was grieving for it.

She didn't think about what she was doing, she just did it. Two seconds later she had her tennis shoes and socks off and had eased herself sideways into the tub on Mac's lap, her legs hanging over the side of the tub, her arms around his neck, her nose plastered against his throat. "I'm so sorry, Mac," she said, her nose burning, her eyes stinging with tears. "I'm so sorry."

At first she thought he was going to push her

away, but his arms closed tight around her and he pulled her close, pressing his cheek tight against hers. She could feel him trembling, feel him struggling to hold back the sobs, until at last they broke free.

She held him close, crooning words that made no sense, offering the comfort of her arms and her love. *Oh, my God. I love him.* It was a stunning realization. A frightening one when she knew his life, now that his future was so uncertain, might very well move in a different direction than hers. But that would not stop what she felt for him. He was another part of her, a part she needed to feel whole inside.

Jewel had no idea how much time had passed when Mac's heaving body finally quieted. He seemed completely relaxed, as though he had accepted the inevitable and was now ready to move beyond it.

"You'd better turn off the water," he said in a voice that was amazingly calm.

Jewel lifted her head and realized the water had reached the rim of the tub and was threatening to spill over. She reached around and shut it off, then turned shyly back to Mac. "I should get off of you and let you finish your bath."

"I wish you wouldn't."

She laughed uncertainly. "What did you have in mind?"

In answer, he lifted her at the waist and rearranged her so she was facing him, her knees on either side of his hips. The extra weight of her legs caused the water to lap over the side of the tub, but Jewel had more important things to think about than a little water on the bathroom floor.

"Mac, do you think we should be doing this now? I mean, what if your leg—"

"Let me worry about my leg," he said.

When she opened her mouth to protest again, he covered it with his hand and said, "I'm fine. Really. Please, Jewel, don't leave me."

She kept her eyes focused on Mac's as he reached for the bottom of her soaked T-shirt and began to lift it up over her head. She raised her arms and let him remove it.

I love him. And I trust him, she realized.

Mac dropped the T-shirt onto the already soaked bath mat and reached behind her for the clasp of her bra. She gripped his shoulders and said nervously, "This is a first for me."

It was a warning and an offering and a prayer. *Please be careful. Please let my body please you. Please let me not be afraid.* She did not ask for what she wanted most. She did not say, *Please love me.* That was something Mac would have to offer on his own.

His eyes were intent on her face as he pulled her lacy, heavy-duty bra off and her Beautiful Breasts—with wonderful big B's, because Mac looked at them that way—fell free. The bra went the way of her T-shirt, and Mac reached out gently, reverently, to cup her breasts in his hands.

"Exquisite," he said, his thumbs flicking the nipples.

Jewel had to remind herself to breathe as sensation streaked from her nipples to a drawstring somewhere deep inside her womb and pulled it up tight. Her hands threaded into the damp hair at Mac's nape as he lowered his head to kiss each breast. His mouth latched onto a nipple and he sucked, gently at first, then more strongly.

Jewel's hips arched instinctively toward him.

"Easy," he said, his hands gripping her hips atop her cutoff jeans. "Slow and easy, Jewel. We have all the time in the world."

"I don't know what to do with my hands," she said anxiously. "Tell me what to do to please you."

He smiled. "You're doing fine."

"I'm not doing anything!" she replied pertly.

He lifted his hips, and she could feel his arousal.

"Oh. Well. I see."

Mac laughed, a rumbly sound, and kissed her quickly on the lips. "I love your innocence," he said, his eyes staring intently into hers. "I want to be the first, Jewel. I am so honored to be the first."

"But—"

He put his fingertips to her lips. "The first," he repeated.

In truth, this situation was so incredibly different from what had happened to her all those years ago, that the past didn't seem real anymore. Mac made her feel innocent, made her feel the joy and excitement—and normal fear—of an untouched woman.

He teased her and touched her and tasted her until they were both wrinkled from the water. And she did the same, enjoying the pleasure of rubbing her breasts against the crisp curls on his chest and returning the favor of kissing and caressing and sucking his nipples—which turned out to be surprisingly sensitive.

"We'd better get out of here," Mac said, "or we're going to turn into prunes."

Jewel felt a little shy standing up and stepping out of the tub. As much as she was tempted to look, she turned her back on Mac as he stood and stepped out of the tub behind her. She had already reached for a towel to cover her breasts, when he took it away from her.

He aligned his body with hers from behind, put his arms around her to cup her breasts and played with her nipples until they were aching and pointy. His mouth teased her throat beneath her ear with kisses, before he latched onto a particular spot and sucked hard enough to make her moan with pleasure.

"I'm only going to touch you," he said, explaining as his hands slid down the front of her, unsnapped her jeans, spread them wide and slid his hand beneath her panties. "To let you feel my hands on you."

She held her breath, expecting the fear to return. But it didn't. She felt only the warmth of his hand against her cooling flesh and the feel of his fingertips probing gently between her thighs. Slowly, carefully, he insinuated one finger inside her.

"Are you all right?" he asked.

"Uh-huh."

She felt his mouth curve into a smile against

her cheek. "I think maybe you'd better breathe," he said.

She exhaled and then gasped a breath of air as his finger slid deeper inside her. "Oh."

He paused. "Did I hurt you?"

"No. I feel..." She searched for the word. *Strange. Full. Achy.* Yes, but more than that. "I feel good," she said. "This feels so right."

"I'm glad." He used his other hand to encourage her to spread her legs, so he would have easier access to her. And slipped another finger inside her.

Her breath was coming in erratic spurts, and she reminded herself to keep breathing.

"Still okay?" he asked.

She nodded, then made a sound when his thumb found the tiny bud at the apex of her thighs and began to caress it. Her knees started to buckle, nature's way of getting her prone, and Mac compensated by putting a strong arm around her midriff and pulling her back tight against him. She could feel his arousal against her buttocks, hard and pulsing.

Instead of being afraid, she was aroused. She was sure she could make love to him this time without running away. She was ready to move forward. She wanted to feel him inside her. "Mac," she said. "I'm not afraid anymore."

"Good," he replied, his voice husky. "Just relax and let me make love to you."

Let me make love to you. It was what she had wanted for a very long time. Jewel let herself fully enjoy what Mac was doing to her—making love to her—without worrying about whether he was *in love* with her. He was as considerate a lover as she could ever have hoped for. He cared for her. That would have to be enough for now.

Mac had one hand inside her jeans, the other tantalizing her nipple, while his mouth teased the flesh at her throat. She writhed against him as her body experienced all the joy and pleasure she had not allowed herself to feel in the past.

As the tension built inside her, she reached out to the pleasure, indulged in it, delighted in it, until she felt herself losing control. "Mac," she said, the fright back in her voice. "What's happening to me?"

"Something wonderful. Let it happen, Jewel. Let me do this for you."

She trusted Mac. As he had trusted her to comfort him. More than that. She loved him.

Jewel gave her body into his hands and was rewarded moments later with a shattering climax, her body shuddering with wave after wave of intense pleasure. "Mac," she gasped. "Mac."

"I know," he said, his voice gentle, his breathing as erratic as hers. "I know."

Jewel felt totally enervated and was barely aware when Mac picked her up in his arms and carried her to her bedroom. He pulled the sheets down on her bed, stood her up long enough to strip the wet cutoffs and panties off her, then tucked her under the covers before she had time to feel embarrassed at being naked.

She expected him to join her. But the last thing she saw before her eyes slid closed was Mac's taut, untanned buttocks as he walked out of the room.

Mac knew that Jewel had expected him to join her in bed, and that he would have been welcome there. He could have eased the ache in his loins and gotten them both over hurdles that had stood in their way for years. He had learned from their recent lovemaking that he had not only the self-control—but the desire—to put Jewel's feelings and needs before his own.

Several things had stopped him from staying. Mac had realized, as he was making love to

Jewel, that he loved her. And not just as a friend, but as an inseparable part of himself. He wanted to spend his life with her. He wanted to plant his seed inside her and help her raise the children they would make together. He wanted to grow old with her.

Which raised a second problem. Mac Macready was another football has-been, who had no idea what he wanted to do with the rest of his life. After the horrific episode with his scarred leg in the tub, there was no denying the truth any longer. He would never play pro football again. Mac had not beaten the odds this time. He had lost.

It was a devastating realization.

If he had not had Jewel to hang on to, he didn't know what he would have done. She had understood his pain and his loss. She had offered comfort without platitudes. She obviously cared for him—even after seeing him at his most vulnerable.

None of the reasons he had for fearing commitment with a woman existed where Jewel was concerned. With her, Mac felt safe making that leap into the unknown, certain he could trust her to be there when he landed.

Which brought him to a third problem. Mac

had no idea whether Jewel loved him merely as a friend or the way he wanted to be loved. As a man. As her lover. As her future husband.

Mac had collected Jewel's clothes before he left the bedroom, wrung out all her wet things and hung them in the bathroom to dry. He had dressed himself in Levi's and a Western shirt, then laid himself down on his bed, his hands behind his head, to think.

On the way up out of the canyon at lunchtime, Jewel had encouraged Brad to tell Mac his interpretation of the primitive drawings on the canyon wall. Mac had listened attentively and heard in Brad's explanation an analogy of what life was like when it was lived in fear of reaching out for dreams. After all, dreams might never come true. You might end up disappointed, or in worse shape than if you had been satisfied with what you already had.

Mac had always believed in pursuing his dreams. He had never been indecisive. But clearly there were moments when old dreams had to be abandoned—and new dreams dreamed. Mac could no longer be a professional football player. So what else did he want to do with his life?

That wasn't an easy question to answer, because Mac had been so determined to regain the use of his scarred leg that he had refused to think about alternatives. Now he must. And he had to factor Jewel, and her commitment to Camp LittleHawk, into the equation.

The idea that rose immediately in his mind was such a simple solution—and yet so revolutionary in terms of how he had intended to spend his life—that Mac felt both excited and cautious about pursuing it. Maybe the best thing to do was to approach Jewel and see what she thought.

He was on his way back to her room when someone knocked hard and fast on the door to the cottage. He hurried to the door and opened it to find Gavin Talbot standing there.

"I think you better get Jewel and come to the boys' bunkhouse," he said. "Brad Templeton has a fever."

Chapter 13

Jewel blamed herself for not recognizing that Brad's flushed face at lunch was caused not only by excitement but also by the fever that signaled the return of his leukemia—and the end of his second remission.

She could barely manage to keep a smile on her face as she belted Brad into the seat of the chartered plane for the short flight back to Dallas Children's Hospital, which was waiting to readmit him. Brad was gripping Mac's football tightly in the crook of one arm. His eyes were feverishly bright, and he had a smile plastered on his face as phony as the one on hers.

Jewel felt Mac's presence at her side. She saw the muscles in his scarred leg as he knelt facing Brad. Mac knew what the end of Brad's remission meant as well as she did. The boy's chances of survival were considerably less now than they had been at the beginning of the week. Mac might very well be bidding Brad Templeton goodbye for the last time.

"Hey, tiger," Mac said, tugging the brim of Brad's cap down playfully. "How's it going?"

Brad readjusted the cap and said, "It's back."

"I know," Mac said. "Remember what I said."

"Yeah. Doctors don't know everything."

Mac nodded soberly. "You keep fighting," he said, his voice low and fierce. He spoke so softly Jewel could barely hear him. "Don't give up. I expect to see you back here next summer. In fact, I expect you to be a counselor someday at a sports camp I'm thinking about starting, where lots of football players like Troy Aikman and Dan Marino and Reggie White and Jerry Rice will come and spend a little time with kids like you."

Jewel wondered where Mac had come up with the idea of a sports camp to encourage Brad. The way Brad's face had lit up, it had certainly been a good idea. She was surprised by the other message Brad had heard in Mac's speech.

"Does that mean you're not gonna play football anymore?" Brad asked.

Mac shook his head. "My leg can't tolerate it."

"So sometimes the doctors *are* right," Brad said.

Jewel watched as Mac gripped Brad's free hand in his and said, "Believe in yourself, and you'll come through fine."

"Time for takeoff, folks," the pilot announced. The nurse who was traveling with Brad was already buckled into her seat.

Mac stood, but Brad held on to his hand and pulled him back down onto his knee. "Goodbye, Mac," he said, a farewell in case he never came back. His chin wobbled and tears welled in his eyes.

"See you soon, Brad," Mac replied. He hugged the boy, who dropped the football and reached up to grab Mac tight around the neck with both hands.

"I don't want to go back to the hospital," Brad said. "Please don't make me leave."

"You have to go. You need help to get well."

"I'm not going to get well. I'm going to die!" Brad cried.

"You'd better not," Mac said severely. "I'm counting on you to come through for me."

Jewel watched as Mac pulled Brad's hands free and reached down to retrieve the football from the floor of the plane and put it back in Mac's arms. "Remember, if I made it, you can make it, too," Mac said.

A tear spilled over as Brad glanced at Jewel for confirmation of Mac's promise.

Her throat was too swollen to speak. She whispered, "Come back soon, Brad," then backed away, keeping the smile on her face as long as she could. It was gone before she reached the door.

Once off the plane, Jewel ran all the way to the van. She had freely chosen to work with kids like Brad, knowing they didn't all make it. With some of them, it was especially hard to let go. Brad's life had seemed so full of possibilities, as Mac's had been all those years ago. Now Mac had lost his dream. And Brad might lose his life.

Jewel felt Mac's arms close around her from behind. He turned her to face the runway, which she saw through a haze of tears, and lifted her arm so she was waving at Brad as the chartered plane took off. Then Mac turned her to face him and closed his arms tightly around her, offering her a comforting shoulder to lay her head on.

"I can't bear it," she said. "First to see you so unhappy, and now Brad..." She couldn't say the word *dying*.

"Brad will make it," Mac said fervently.

"How can you be so sure?" she sobbed.

"I know these things," he said. "Besides, I'm going to need him when I start my sports camp for kids with cancer."

It took a moment for what he said to sink in. When it did, Jewel backed out of his arms and stared at him in shocked disbelief. "I thought you made that up for Brad's sake."

"Nope. It's for real." He opened the door of the van and hustled her inside, then got into the driver's seat and started up the vehicle.

"Why haven't I heard about this sports camp before?" Jewel asked, wiping the tears from her eyes.

He grinned at her. "Because I just thought it up this afternoon."

"Oh."

''I wanted to talk to you about it before I went much further with the idea. What do you think about it?''

Jewel's first thought was that it would take Mac away from Hawk's Pride. That was selfish. What Mac planned to do would help a great many children. ''I think what you're planning is one of the noblest, most considerate—''

The van veered to the berm and skidded to a halt. Before Jewel could say another word, Mac's arms were around her and his mouth had covered hers.

She had no time to think, only to feel. What she felt was overflowing love for this man who had so much strength, yet had let her see him when he was at his most vulnerable. She reached out to touch Mac's face tenderly, to thank him for being who he was.

He broke off the kiss abruptly, and she was caught by his gaze, which promised so much— hope, happiness and something else she was afraid to name, because she wanted it so much she feared she had merely wished it there.

''Look at me like that too long, love, and you're liable to get what you want right here and now, instead of when we get back to the cottage.''

Jewel stared into Mac's blue eyes, her heart pounding. Had he really called her *love?* Had he said they were going to be making love in a few minutes? He didn't repeat himself, merely started up the van and pulled back onto the road.

Jewel suddenly realized why Mac had reached out to her physically. Making love was an act to reaffirm life in the presence of death. *We can reach out for joy. We still have our lives ahead of us, whatever those lives may bring. This offer of lovemaking has nothing to do with Mac actually loving me. It's a reaction to Brad's illness.* She couldn't disagree with Mac's motive. Or with wanting to be held close, no matter what the reason. She wasn't going to deny him, or herself, the lovemaking he had promised.

''Tell me more about the camp,'' she said to break the strained silence.

''There isn't any more to tell,'' he replied. ''It's just an idea right now. Do you have any suggestions?''

''Where do you plan to locate it?''

He frowned. ''That's a problem. I probably have enough money left from my signing bonus with the Tornadoes to advertise the place and hire help for the first year. But I doubt whether I have enough to buy a piece of land and build buildings. Any suggestions?''

Jewel would have offered her facilities immediately, if she had thought he would accept. His explanation seemed to suggest he would be perfectly happy to open his camp right here.

The way he was looking at her, his heart in his eyes, gave her the courage to speak. ''Camp LittleHawk belongs to my mother, but she's said it can be mine whenever I want it. I think having a sports program here—with famous football players participating on occasion—would be a welcome addition.''

Mac smiled at her, and she felt her throat swell with emotion. ''Thanks, Jewel. Incorporating my idea with what you've already established at Camp LittleHawk would please me very much.''

They had arrived back at the cottage, and Mac quickly left the van and came around to help Jewel out. He took her hand and practically dragged her into the cottage. She realized why he was in such a hurry when, the instant they were inside with the door closed behind them, he pulled her into his arms and pressed her to him from breast to thigh. The evidence of his desire was hard to miss.

"I love you, Jewel."

The way he blurted it out seemed to surprise him as much as it surprised her. His eyes looked wary, as though he wished he hadn't spoken.

She shoved back the hurt and said, "It's all right, Mac. You don't have to say things like that."

The wary look disappeared, and his jaw firmed. "I don't *have* to say it. I *want* to say it. I love you, Jewel. I think I have for a very long time. I was afraid to do anything about it, afraid even to admit it, I think, because of all the bad things that happened when I loved someone in the past.

"What's happened to Brad made me realize I don't want to wait any longer. Life is too precious to waste a single day of it. I love you," he repeated. "And I want to make love with you."

Jewel took a deep breath and let it out. If he could find the courage to speak, so could she. "I love you, too, Mac. I've been afraid to tell you, afraid you wouldn't feel the same way. Afraid—''

She never got a chance to finish. His mouth captured hers at the same time he reached down to lift her up and carry her toward his bedroom.

Mac laid Jewel down on his bed as gently as he could and sat down beside her. He hadn't expected his courage to desert him, but it seemed for a moment that he wouldn't be able to go through with what he had planned.

It was late in the day, and the growing dusk gave everything in the room a soft, rosy glow. Jewel had never looked more beautiful to him. Or more trusting.

He had never been more nervous. Or frightened.

Think of her feelings, not your own.

''Are you all right?'' he asked.

''More than all right,'' she said, a tender smile on her lips. ''Kiss me please, Mac.''

He had never been more gentle, more tender, more considerate of a woman. He brushed his mouth against hers, teased her lips, nipped at her and eased his tongue into her mouth to taste her. He felt her growing desire, her growing urgency to touch and taste in return.

He put his arms around her and pulled her close, feeling the tips of her breasts turn as pointy as pebbles when they made contact with his chest. "Would you like me to undress you?" he asked.

"I'd rather undress you," she said with a mischievous smile.

Mac was surprised, but when he thought about it, it seemed like a good idea. If he was undressed while she was still clothed, she would have the opportunity of escaping anytime she didn't feel comfortable. "Okay," he said. "Where would you like to start?"

She got off the bed and said, "Sit back on the bed, so I can take off your boots." She turned her back to him and tugged at each of his boot heels, while he gave her a shove with the opposite foot to help get the cowboy boots off. Then she pulled off his socks and said, "Stand up."

He stood barefoot on the wooden floor and watched as she slowly pulled his Western shirt out of his jeans and unsnapped the snaps, one at a time from the top downward. He wasn't wearing an undershirt, and she kissed her way down his chest. He was quivering by the time she reached the soft line of down that disappeared into his jeans.

When she ran her tongue around his navel, he nearly jumped out of his skin. "Good God," he muttered.

"You didn't like it?" she asked, looking up into his face.

He shoved both hands through his hair in agitation. "I'm about to explode because of it," he admitted.

Jewel smiled. "That's good, don't you think?"

Patience. Patience. Patience. He said it like a mantra, hoping he could endure her innocent exploration. He bit the inside of his cheek when she undid his belt, pulled it through the loops of his jeans and let it drop to the floor.

She unbuttoned the top button of his Levi's and began to lower the zipper. Her hand brushed against his tumescence, and he grabbed her wrist to avoid disaster. He wanted desperately to tell her it was the first time for him, but the words wouldn't come out. Instead he said, "It's been a while for me, Jewel. I don't want to disappoint you."

"What about Eve?" she asked.

He had forgotten all about Eve. "Nothing happened with her," he said.

"But you were gone so long that first night. And when you met her in Dallas, I thought—"

"She never turned me on," Mac blurted. "I couldn't... I didn't... Damn it, Jewel! You know what I'm trying to say." He could feel the heat rising on his throat. He couldn't believe what he had just confessed.

He waited for the laughter, and it came—a warm, happy sound that made his heart soar.

"Oh, Mac," Jewel said, her dark brown eyes bright with joy. "If you only knew how much I've wanted to hear you say those exact words— or something very like them."

"You have?"

"I've been terribly jealous," she admitted. Jewel rubbed her cheek against the curls on his chest, then kissed him, sending goose bumps skittering across his flesh. "I'm so glad," she said. "I've wanted you all to myself." The smile returned as she said, "And now I've got you."

She pushed his shirt off his shoulders until it caught at his wrists, effectively making him a prisoner. Instead of releasing the snaps, she shot him a grin and said, "You're my captive now. I can do whatever I want with you."

He leaned down to kiss her, and she stepped back and wagged her finger at him.

"Oh, no, you don't. I'm going to be doing the kissing and touching." She reached down and cupped him with her hand.

"You're going to kill me," Mac said through gritted teeth.

"You don't like it?" she teased.

"You know I like it," he retorted. "I like it so much I'm about to burst."

"Good," she said. "Now you stand right there while I undress."

Mac's eyes went wide when Jewel began a striptease in front of him. No woman had ever removed a T-shirt, bra, jeans and panties quite so seductively.

Don't think of yourself. Think of her.

Mac's pulse was pounding in his temples—and elsewhere. His whole body quivered with excitement.

"You're so beautiful," he said when she was naked at last.

She touched the crisscrossing scars on her face and the more visible scar on her thigh, where the operations to mend her leg had been performed. "You don't mind?"

He solved the problem of the imprisoning shirt by pulling his arms up over his head and using the shirt between his hands as a chain to encircle her and pull her close. "All I see is a beautiful, desirable woman."

She made a sound of pleasure when her breasts were finally pillowed against his naked chest. He spread his legs and urged her between them. Her hands curved around his waist and ventured up his back all the way to his nape. His blood raced as her hands caressed him.

He shuddered out a breath. *Think of her. Give her pleasure. Make it good for her. Don't think about yourself.*

He lowered his mouth to hers, sealing them together, mimicking the sex act with his tongue. The sounds she made in her throat caused his groin to tighten even more—if that was possible. He pushed against her and felt the heat of her through the denim as she rubbed her mound against him.

"I never knew it could feel so good," she whispered. "I never imagined how wonderful it would be."

He kissed her eyes and cheeks and nose before he reached her mouth again. She kissed him back eagerly, her tongue thrusting into his mouth, tasting him, dueling with him as he sought to return the favor.

Mac had forgotten about his jeans. She obviously had not. He felt her hands on the zipper again, and this time he let her lower it and reach inside.

"Okay?" she asked.

Think of her. Think of her. "Okay," he rasped.

But if she thought she was going to have it all her way, she was wrong. When Jewel reached for him, Mac got rid of his shirt and reached for her. He slipped two fingers inside her quickly, before she could protest, and settled his thumb on the tiny nub that was the source of so much delight.

"I can't...concentrate on you...when you're doing that...to me..." she panted.

His body was hard, pulsing in an agony of delight. It was a good thing she was not more experienced, although her innocence was likely to be his undoing.

He concentrated on bringing Jewel to a climax, focusing his attention on kissing her, touching her, pleasing her. Soon her hand was lax against him, her eyes closed, her jaw clenched as the pleasure overtook her. She leaned into him with her hips and arched her body toward him, making it easy for him to kiss her breasts, to suckle them and to tease them with his teeth and tongue.

Sweat beaded on his forehead, as he watched the play of expressions on her face. The rapture. The delight. The confusion as her body tightened more and more, as he pushed her higher and higher. The ecstasy as her body rippled with pleasure. And the love, as she looked up at him from hooded eyes and rose on tiptoe to find his mouth with hers and thank him with a kiss.

He picked her up, pulled down his bedcovers and laid her on the sheet. Her eyes had already slid closed before he pulled off his jeans and briefs and slid into bed beside her. He wrapped his arms around her and pulled her back into the hollow of his belly. He lay there bone hard and unsatisfied—but very pleased with himself.

He had brought Jewel to climax twice now and managed to control his own urgent need. Surely it would not be so difficult to put himself inside her and do it so she would not recognize his inexperience. She seemed to have put completely out of her mind what had happened six years ago.

He wished she were awake now. He wished he did not have to wait. If he could just make love to her this instant, he knew everything would be fine. But she seemed perfectly satisfied to lie beside him. She did not seem the least bit interested in any more touching or kissing.

Mac got the first hint of his error when he felt Jewel's hand sliding up his thigh, headed for the barely relaxed, unsatisfied part of him.

"Jewel? What's going on?"

She turned in his arms to face him. Her eyes were two shiny spots in the darkness. "I want to make love to you, Mac."

"We just—"

"I want you to put yourself inside me as deep as you can. I want to make you feel as wonderful as you've made me feel."

Mac swallowed hard. He felt like crying. "God, Jewel. Now?"

"Now." She touched him, and his body stood at rigid attention. She lay back and urged him over her.

She didn't have to urge him very hard.

For a moment she hesitated, and Mac realized she was remembering the past. This was the way he had found her with Harvey Barnes. Harvey was on top, and she was helpless beneath him. Like Harvey, Mac was stronger. He could do to her whatever he wanted.

Mac saw her rising fear and said, "It's me, Jewel."

Her whole body relaxed, and she smiled up at him sweetly. "I know, Mac. Love me, please. And let me love you."

Patience. Patience.

Patience went out the window the instant his body reached the entrance to hers. Mac tried to go slow, but she was wet and hot, and he wanted to be inside her so bad, that it took only three brief thrusts before he was buried deep inside her.

Mac paused, his weight on his elbows, his hips cradled in hers, and looked down, ashamed of his haste and afraid of what he would see on her face. "Jewel?"

"I'm fine," she said, her eyes glowing, her fingertips caressing his cheeks. "I'm wonderful."

It was all right. She couldn't tell it was his first time…because it was also the first time for her, he realized.

It was easy then, to think of her and not himself. "I don't want to hurt you," he said.

In response, she lifted her knees on either side of him, then wrapped her legs around his buttocks, seating him even more deeply inside her.

"My God," he muttered. "Jewel, I…" He withdrew and thrust as slowly and gently as he could, but the inevitable urge to mate, to put his seed inside her, drove him to move faster. When she lifted her hips and pushed back, the friction created unbelievably exquisite sensations.

Go slow. Slow down. Wait for her.

He saw Jewel's face through a haze of desire, heard her guttural sounds of pleasure and finally felt her body, slick and wet beneath him, begin to convulse.

Her body squeezed him, wringing pleasure beyond anything he could have imagined. He arched his head backward in an agony of joy as he spilled his seed inside her. His body pulsed, emptying itself in powerful thrusts before he lowered himself to lie beside her and wrapped her in his arms.

His breathing was ragged, his blood still pumping so hard it throbbed in his veins. He could not find breath for words, and would not have known what to say if he could have spoken.

"Thank you, Mac," Jewel whispered, snuggling close. "No man could have made me feel more lovely...or more loved."

Mac kissed her on the temple, a wordless thanks for saying what he had not been able to find words to express. The pleasure of this first time for him was all the sweeter, knowing she was happy.

Mac thought of all the women he could have made love to and had not. All the sex he had turned down in those early years, which had put him in the position of making love for the first time to the very woman he hoped to marry. As far as Mac was concerned, that meant Jewel was the only woman he would ever make love with.

Maybe he should have felt deprived. He did not.

Intuitively Mac knew that sex with a stranger—or even an acquaintance, would not have been as earth-shattering, or as bone-melting, as his experience with Jewel. Without the love he felt for her—and the love she felt for him in return—the sex act would not have brought him nearly so much joy.

"What are you thinking?" Jewel murmured.

"How much I enjoyed making love to you," he replied with a smile.

She kept her eyes lowered, and she was obviously struggling to speak as she said, "Considering the experience of the other women you must have slept with, I can't imagine my first efforts were much to shout about."

"Will you marry me?"

Mac had meant to distract her from a discussion of his sexual experience, and the proposal worked. But not in the way he had hoped.

"Does that mean you were satisfied?" she said, arching a brow. "I don't want to spend my life wondering how I stack up against the competition," she said wryly.

"I'm never going to be comparing you to anyone else," he muttered.

"Why don't I believe you?"

"Believe me."

"How can I believe you?" she said, rising to her elbow and staring down at him. "Are you telling me you never found a single other woman who was more appealing to you in bed than me?"

"That's exactly what I'm saying," he retorted, sitting up abruptly. "Because there were no other women."

She sat up just as quickly to face him, and the sheet dropped to her waist, exposing her breasts. "You're kidding, right?"

The sight of her nipples, full and rosy, set his pulse to galloping. "No man would kid about something like that. Until a few minutes ago I was a virgin. Now damn it, will you or won't you marry me?"

He had known she would laugh if she ever found out the truth. But he had never expected such gentle laughter. Such joyful laughter. Such loving laughter.

Jewel pushed him onto his back and straddled him with only the sheet between them. She leaned down, her lips close to his and said, "Oh, yes, my darling. I will most definitely marry you."

"It doesn't bother you that I don't have more experience in bed?" he demanded.

She chuckled. "Why should it? This way we can both learn exactly what pleases us. For instance, do you like it when I bite your earlobe like this?''

He shivered at the searing sensation of pleasure.

''Or would you rather I kissed this spot below your ear?''

Mac groaned. He had switched their positions and had her beneath him in two seconds flat. ''I like it all,'' he said, nipping her earlobe and then kissing her below the ear, feeling the frisson of pleasure that rippled through her. ''Just so long as I'm doing it with you.''

''Well, then,'' she said, smiling up at him, ''why don't we practice making a baby?''

Mac laughed, then cheerfully indulged the future mother of his children.

Epilogue

Jewel sat in a rocker on the covered porch of the two-story Victorian house Mac had built for them. It stood on Hawk's Pride land her father had given them as a wedding present four years ago. Jewel had wanted a white house with lots of gingerbread trim with morning glories entwined in it, and that was exactly what she had.

She sighed with pleasure every time she looked around her. This was her favorite place to be these days. She was nursing her second son, while the first, blond-haired, blue-eyed, three-year-old Evan, played with a football at her feet.

"Daddy!" Evan cried, leaping up as Mac appeared around the corner of the house.

Mac opened his arms when he reached the foot of the steps that led up to the front door, and Evan launched himself into his father's arms. The two looked very much alike, down to the twin dimples in their cheeks.

"Welcome home," Jewel said with a smile.

"It's good to be home," Mac replied, settling into the rocker beside her with Evan on his lap. "How's Dustin?"

"Hungry, as always."

"I can see why he enjoys dinner so much," Mac said with a teasing smile, as he eyed the breast that provided his son's nourishment.

Jewel blushed. Even after four years of marriage, Mac talked about her breasts as though they were the best gift he had ever been given. "How did your trip go?" she asked.

"I got two Pro-Bowl quarterbacks, a former Heisman Trophy winner and a record-setting kicker to commit to a week each at Camp Little-Hawk."

"Fabulous!" Jewel said. "I knew you could do it! What about the fund-raiser?"

Jewel had been as surprised as Mac when

Andy Dennison suggested they raise money for Mac's sports camp from the public. The Camp LittleHawk fund-raiser had become a highlight on the sports calendar and football players from around the league were delighted to be invited to participate.

"Everything is in place," Mac said. "Andy says he thinks we can double what we made last year."

"That'll mean we can build another couple of bunkhouses," Jewel said. "And hire the help we'll need to staff them."

Mac nodded and set his rocker to moving. "How were things around here while I was gone?"

"The high school-age summer counselors arrived yesterday for their week of training."

"Did he come?"

Jewel smiled. "He came."

Mac leaned his head back and turned his face away, but Jewel had already seen the tears that leaped to his eyes.

"He's been in remission for three years, Mac. Don't you think it's safe now to admit how much you like the kid?"

Mac turned back to her and reached out to take her hand in his. "I suppose it is."

"I thought so. That's why I asked him over for dinner tonight."

"What?"

"You can come out now, Brad," Jewel said.

The screen door opened, and Brad Templeton stepped onto the front porch. "Hi, Mac."

Mac rose and set Evan down.

It was questionable which of the two men moved first, but the instant they met, they wrapped their arms around each other and hugged tight.

Neither of them said anything, but if they were as moved as Jewel was, they were both too emotional to speak.

Mac recovered first, pushed Brad an arm's length away and said, "Let me look at you. How old are you now?"

"Sixteen," Brad said.

"You've gotten taller."

"You look the same."

Mac pulled off the New York Mets baseball cap and tousled Brad's dark hair. "Looks like you need a trim."

Brad grabbed the ball cap and tugged it down.

"Now that I've got a little hair, I'm not about to cut it off. Besides, the chicks like it like this."

Mac laughed as he put an arm around Brad's shoulder and headed back toward Jewel. "Just remember," he said, pointing his thumb at Jewel, "this one's taken."

"I thought you had the hots for her," Brad said, winking at Jewel. "Guess I was right."

Mac laughed, then sobered. "I'm so glad you made it back here," he said, his voice breaking with emotion.

"I owe it all to you. I kept on fighting, like you said. And here I am."

The screen door slammed again and Jewel's brother Colt appeared on the front porch, tossing a football from hand to hand. At eighteen, his shoulders had broadened, and he had grown a few more inches. His hair was too long, and his face held a perpetual look of defiance. "If the reunion is over, I promised to throw Brad a few passes."

"Sure," Mac said, giving Brad a nudge in Colt's direction. "Let's see what kind of speed you have, Brad."

Mac returned to the rocker and settled down,

picking up Evan again and holding him in his lap.

"Football," Evan said, pointing to Colt and Brad.

"Yep. Someday you're going to be playing, sport. But right now we're going to watch your uncle Colt and my friend Brad."

As the two of them watched Brad run in a zigzagging pattern, Jewel said, "Colt finally told Dad he's been accepted to the Air Force Academy."

Mac missed seeing Colt throw the football, because his attention had switched to Jewel. "What did Zach say?"

"He was angry that Colt hadn't said anything to him before now about wanting to go into the Air Force."

"And?"

"They're not speaking at the moment."

"What did Rebecca say?" Mac asked, his eyes back on Colt.

"Mom was hurt by all the secrecy. And she's afraid for Colt, because what he wants to do will put him in the path of danger."

Mac's mouth turned up wryly. "That shouldn't surprise her. Colt has led a pretty reckless life the past four years. It's a wonder he got through high school alive."

"I can't help thinking how unhappy Colt must have been all these years, knowing he was going to disappoint Dad and hurt Mom when he finally told them the truth about what he wanted to do with his life."

"Who'd have thought it," Mac said, watching the perfect spiraling pass Colt had thrown land gently in Brad's outstretched arms. "He would have made one hell of a pro quarterback."

"Apparently he'll play football for the Air Force Academy," Jewel said. "When he's done, he plans to fly jets."

Mac brushed his thumb across Jewel's knuckles, sending a frisson of pleasure streaking up her arm. "Do you think Colt would talk to me?"

"I'm sure he could use an ear to listen," Jewel said. "I've invited him for dinner, too."

Mac smiled. "Have I told you lately how much I love you?"

"It's been twenty-four hours, at least."

"I love you, Jewel." Mac raised her hand and kissed her palm.

Jewel found herself breathless as she met his avid gaze. "It's time for another lesson in the bedroom," she said.

"Oh? What are we learning this time?"

"How to make a baby *girl*," Jewel said.

"Sounds interesting," Mac said. "When does class start?"

"Right after the dinner dishes are done," Jewel said, "and you talk to Colt and he drives Brad back to Camp LittleHawk and we get these two into bed."

"I'll be there," Mac promised with a grin. "This is a lesson I don't want to miss."

Jewel laughed. "Just get it right this time, or you're liable to find yourself with a whole football team before we're through."

"I wouldn't mind," Mac said softly. "As long as we get at least one girl who looks just like you."

Before Jewel could answer, a football came flying onto the porch, and Mac and Evan abandoned her to play football with the two teenagers.

Jewel fingered the soft curls at Dustin's nape and brushed her hand across his baby-soft cheek. She was looking forward to Mac's inventive lovemaking tonight. Knowing his determination to do everything to the best of his ability, it was bound to be a delightful adventure, full of fun and laughter.

Only this time, she would have the last laugh. Jewel's smile grew as she imagined the look on

Mac's face when she told him—after the lesson, of course—that his daughter was already on the way.

*   *   *   *   *

This Christmas,
share in the joy of the holiday season
with Rolleen Whitelaw and
Gavin Talbot's love story,

A HAWK'S WAY CHRISTMAS,

a brand new novella by Joan Johnston
in Silhouette's hardcover
Christmas anthology,
A Lone Star Christmas.

And next year watch for
the moving story of Colt Whitelaw
and the woman he loves in

THE SUBSTITUTE GROOM

coming only from
Silhouette books.

Share in the joy of yuletide romance with brand-new
stories by two of the genre's most beloved writers

DIANA PALMER
and
JOAN JOHNSTON
in

LONE STAR CHRISTMAS

Diana Palmer and Joan Johnston share their favorite
Christmas anecdotes and personal stories in this
special hardbound edition.

Diana Palmer delivers an irresistible spin-off of her
LONG, TALL TEXANS series and Joan Johnston crafts an
unforgettable new chapter to **HAWK'S WAY** in this wonderful
keepsake edition celebrating the holiday season. So
perfect for gift giving, you'll want one for yourself...and
one to give to a special friend!

Available in November at your favorite retail outlet!

Only from

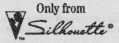
Silhouette®

Take 4 bestselling love stories FREE

Plus get a FREE surprise gift!

Special Limited-time Offer

Mail to Silhouette Reader Service™

3010 Walden Avenue
P.O. Box 1867
Buffalo, N.Y. 14240-1867

YES! Please send me 4 free Silhouette Desire® novels and my free surprise gift. Then send me 6 brand-new novels every month, which I will receive months before they appear in bookstores. Bill me at the low price of $2.90 each plus 25¢ delivery and applicable sales tax, if any.* That's the complete price and a savings of over 10% off the cover prices—quite a bargain! I understand that accepting the books and gift places me under no obligation ever to buy any books. I can always return a shipment and cancel at any time. Even if I never buy another book from Silhouette, the 4 free books and the surprise gift are mine to keep forever.

225 BPA A3UU

Name	(PLEASE PRINT)	
Address	Apt. No.	
City	State	Zip

This offer is limited to one order per household and not valid to present Silhouette Desire® subscribers. *Terms and prices are subject to change without notice.
Sales tax applicable in N.Y.

UDES-696   ©1990 Harlequin Enterprises Limited

"For smoldering sensuality and exceptional storytelling, Elizabeth Lowell is incomparable."
—*Romantic Times*

New York Times bestselling author

ELIZABETH LOWELL

LAURA CHANDLER
has come home a
woman—wiser and stronger
than the day she left.

CARSON BLACKRIDGE
is waiting—determined
to win Laura back for all
the right reasons.

Sweet Wind, Wild Wind

Even as Laura begins to trust in the love she has denied,
the fear that history is repeating itself grows within her
and she's afraid.... Afraid she'll make the same mistakes.

Available August 1997
at your favorite retail outlet.

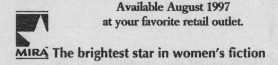

MIRA The brightest star in women's fiction

National Bestselling Author

MARY LYNN BAXTER

"Ms. Baxter's writing…strikes every chord within the female spirit."
—Sandra Brown

LONE STAR *Heat*

SHE is Juliana Reed, a prominent broadcast journalist whose television show is about to be syndicated. Until the murder…

HE is Gates O'Brien, a high-ranking member of the Texas Rangers, determined to forget about his ex-wife. He's onto something bad….

Juliana and Gates are ex-spouses, unwillingly involved in an explosive circle of political corruption, blackmail and murder.

In order to survive, they must overcome the pain of the past…and the very demons that drove them apart.

Available in September 1997 at your favorite retail outlet.

MIRA The brightest star in women's fiction

Look us up on-line at:http://www.romance.net

KASEY MICHAELS

Continues the twelve-book
series—36 HOURS—in
August 1997 with
Book Two

STRANGE BEDFELLOWS

When the raging storm stranded single father Sean Frame
and guidance counselor Cassandra Mercer together, rivals
became lovers as Cassandra offered him the one thing she
held dear—her innocence. Once rescued, would they become
rivals once again? Or would their impulsive act of passion lead
to a lifetime promise?

For Sean and Cassandra and *all* the residents of Grand
Springs, Colorado, the storm-induced blackout was just the
beginning of 36 Hours that changed *everything!* You won't
want to miss a single book.

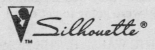

Silhouette®

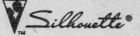
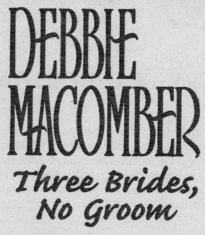